*Dedicated to the people I remember when
I walk around the Botanical Gardens*

SURVIVOR

One mysterious death on the Ultimate Bushcraft adventure holiday is tragic, but a second, then a third is suspicious . . . But who can you trust when everyone around you is a suspect? As numbers dwindle, the chances of survival plummet. Staying alive has never seemed so guilty.

Nobody is safe . . .

Books by Tom Hoyle

Thirteen

Spiders

Survivor

SURVIVOR

TOM HOYLE

MACMILLAN CHILDREN'S BOOKS

First published 2015 by Macmillan Children's Books
an imprint of Pan Macmillan
The Smithson, 6 Briset Street, London EC1M 5NR
EU representative: Macmillan Publishers Ireland Limited,
Mallard Lodge, Lansdowne Village, Dublin 4
Associated companies throughout the world
www.panmacmillan.com

ISBN 978-1-4472-8675-2

13

A CIP catalogue record for this book is available from
the British Library.

Printed and bound by CPI Group (UK) Ltd, Croydon CR0 4YY

PROLOGUE

This is everything as it happened. So you understand what it was like – how difficult it was. I can't remember it all *exactly*, what people said, how they looked . . . But it's close enough to the truth, I think.

George Fleet

CHAPTER 1
(NEARLY A YEAR BEFORE):
THE FIRST PART OF GEORGE
FLEET'S STATEMENT

I'll tell the story from the beginning. Right from the very start.

Yes, I'll be honest. I don't tell lies – at least not unless I really *have* to. I'll just say it as it was.

None of it would have happened if I hadn't missed a bus.

I arrived just in time to see the red lights of the number 6 slip away into the distance. When the next one arrived, I headed upstairs to avoid a gang of boys I didn't recognize. I sat halfway down on the right to avoid empty lager cans near the front. Isn't it weird? After everything, I still remember little things like rolling lager cans.

So, you see, I was more or less level with the window of the flat when the bus stopped to pick up some passengers by the war memorial.

I had glanced at the football scores on my phone and was about to text Louis – who is still my best friend – when I realized that the cloudy red light in the flat's window wasn't a reflection of the setting sun, but flames. I saw smoke creeping out from under the eaves of the roof.

I said, 'That building's on fire!' It was more to myself at the time, but even when I shouted people looked away, thinking I was crazy. They didn't even check to see if there were flames. People don't see danger when it's right in front of their noses.

As I stared at the flat, the net curtain moved and a hand slammed against the windowpane.

Afterwards, when I heard my voice on the emergency-services recording, I was amazed at how calm I sounded. My voice still had that low boom that I hate, but I basically sounded cool and in control. Not that I can remember making the call or advising them to send an ambulance and *at least three fire engines*. Everyone said that it was remarkable, that bit about the three fire engines – they seemed to think it was stranger than what I actually *did*. I suppose I imagined three fire engines blocking the road. Everyone laughed when they found out that I'd said *excuse me* to the people on the bus's stairs as I pushed past. 'Excuse me, but that building's on fire.'

I didn't ever really *decide* to help; it just happened, like I was sliding down a slope, unable to stop myself.

There was a bit in the newspaper about how I left my rucksack with the driver and asked an old guy to stop the traffic. If I left my rucksack with the driver, I must have already decided to go inside the building. But I wasn't thinking. I was just pulled towards the flat as though a magnet was drawing me on.

'Fire – up there!' I hollered.

A man shouted at me while I pounded on the door. 'What the hell are you doing, lad?'

'Fire!' I pointed up at the window, still calm, just *urgent*. 'There's someone up there!' I didn't panic, even then. I sort of saw myself from the outside, like I was an actor, like I couldn't be hurt, not badly hurt, anyway.

All of a sudden, everyone seemed to grasp that there was a disaster happening. A big guy, white T-shirt stretched over muscles, was passing at *exactly* the right moment. He shoved his shoulder against the door twice, there was a crack and a snap and it splintered open. Swirling smoke crept towards us, like fingers reaching for the fresh air. Sorry for the metaphor – or simile – whatever – I know that this isn't an essay for an English lesson – but I really saw it like that at the time. Fingers. I thought of horror-movie fingers.

'Open the window!' people shouted. 'Break the glass and jump down!' others yelled. At the time, no one was sure why the woman didn't open the window properly, but later we knew that she couldn't, that it had been painted shut. The words 'she's got a kid' filled the street and my brain. Flecks of glass showered down on us and there was a desperate high-pitched scream – a nails-down-the-blackboard screech – followed by coughing and spluttering.

The big guy who'd knocked the door down raced into the building first.

I went in after him. I had thought before about doing heroic things, but they never involved dashing into a burning building. I had imagined sword fights, light-sabre battles (I feel embarrassed writing that), flying an aeroplane into a war zone, standing up to bullies against improbable odds (yet I avoided those boys at the back of the bus: some hero!), but I didn't think of any of this when I went in.

I went in because . . . I suppose I would have felt bad if I hadn't. I went in because it was automatic. Because I heard them say 'she's got a kid'. I didn't think that I was only a kid myself; I was fifteen at the time. I'm only sixteen now, of course, though it feels like longer than a year since it happened. *Much longer.*

'Where do you think you're going?' someone shouted behind me. 'Stop being an idiot!'

The big guy had stormed ahead and was standing next

to the young panicking woman when I followed him into the flat. He was trying to drag her away from the window, but she fought against him, slapping and screaming, determined to keep her baby next to the small pane she'd managed to smash – and what little fresh air there was.

'Jump down!' I heard from outside. 'We'll catch you!' A large group had gathered below and were ready to catch anyone who fell. They didn't understand about the window. You see – people outside, looking in, don't always understand.

The room was hot. It was skin-reddeningly hot – only just bearable, and flames were leaping up from the sofa and running up the wall. But it's the smoke that kills, they said; the firemen told us later that flames are there as a warning for the smoke.

Unable to get close to the window, I was surrounded by the fumes and held my breath.

The big guy was the true hero. He smashed the rest of the glass then pulled the baby from his mother. 'No,' she gasped and coughed, 'don't throw him – he'll die.' She still fought to stay in the man's way despite her confusion. 'Give him back,' she mumbled.

I took the baby off him. The kid was heavier than I expected, and not moving. I ran off immediately, crouching down to avoid the worst of the smoke, breath held, baby pressed to my chest, while behind me his mother still fought the other guy, delirious with panic and confusion and the effects of the fumes.

It was, of course, water that saved my life. Not the water from hoses, those were still six or seven minutes away, but a lifetime of swimming, breath-holding competitions and diving off piers and rocks. I held my breath throughout as the poisonous smoke surrounded me.

And so I became a hero. 'Saint George to the Rescue' was the headline on the front page of the local paper, and similar puns on my name were made in the national press. I was on the TV. I had saved a baby's life. The big guy had saved both mother and baby, but he got second billing.

Imagine being responsible for saving someone's life. But it was just chance – the bus stopped, I looked out of the window, someone tough was passing. But without these chances the first of a terrible series of dominoes would not have fallen. And I wonder, right now, whether it might actually have been better for me not to have saved that kid's life at all.

[Here ends the first part of George Fleet's statement]

THE OTHER CHAPTER 1
(SAID IN THE HOUR BEFORE):
HIM

Shut up! Now it's MY turn to speak. If you know what's good for you, you'll listen.

Just you and me. At **THE END** of the story.

You know that this is not a happy ending. No. Not happy FOR YOU at all.

But you <u>deserve</u> an <u>un</u>happy ending.

And they all lived <u>un</u>happily ever after. Because that's what they **DESERVED**.

THE END

I've done quite a bit, haven't I?

Haven't I?

Quite a few have

DIED.

They **deserved** it.

<u>Bastards</u>.

Useless bastards.

Mostly useless. Mostly bastards. One or the other, anyway.

9

And all of it is <u>your</u> fault.

TIME FOR JUSTICE.

DING DONG.

JUSTICE CALLING.

Mmmmmmmmmmmmmmmmmmmmmmmmmmmmm.

I always knew he was a bad person: that's what you're thinking. I can see it on your pretty – your pretty <u>pathetic</u> – face.

Who are you kidding? You don't know me. You don't know <u>*anything*</u>.

You don't know WHO I am or WHAT I am or what I DID.

You don't understand because you are so wrapped up in your own life, so far up your own arse that you don't know anything about anyone. Least of all me.

But now you know that it was *me*.

Yeah. Yeah. It was **ME!**

Oh I'm so sorry! Please let me cry about it. Please help me.

No. I'm not sorry. They deserved it.

And are you so different to me anyway?

That's why I really hate people like you. You do what you can for <u>yourself</u>, and would kill for <u>your</u> own family, which means for YOURSELF. It's all about **you**.

We're all in it for ourselves.

We're all animals. I'm just freer. I'm the animal that

roams where it wants and kills when it wants. The KING of the jungle.

Who doesn't like winning? And what's killing? It's the ultimate victory. No one persecutes the lion because he kills. I'm the LION. Even the cute little robin kills worms. Stick that on your Christmas cards: THIS ANIMAL IS A KILLER.

You think I'm *evil*. But that's a LIE. *Evil* doesn't mean anything. It just means that I'm different to you. Freer (I <u>love</u> that word, free, free, FREE); more free than you.

Now that we have some time, let me tell you about the first person I did in. *Are you sitting comfortably?*

It was JUSTICE, this one. *Once upon a time* there was a boy who came into class. He had hair like yours. But that's just a coincidence.

Anyway, you're distracting me. You shouldn't do that. If you do it again, I'll hurt you.

In the beginning there was a boy. He came in when he shouldn't have, into the class, and started smiling and showing off and <u>sapping my energy</u>. He was like a parasite, living off us, feeding on us, just so that HE could laugh and FORCE others to laugh – which was MY job. So it was JUSTICE what I did.

I suppose you want to know how I did it.

Easier than A, B, C.

11

Miss Rogers, Miss Rogers – that's me speaking, very sweetly – *he just stepped out, Miss Rogers. Into the road, Miss Rogers.*

And we were free of him. Free of the bastard cuckoo who had invaded the nest.

I hated him.

But there's one name I hate more.

GEORGE. GEORGE FLEET.

I remember that first moment I saw GEORGE in the airport. Pathetic.

I think I should stop and let you think about all of this. I'm suddenly a bit tired. You're making me tired. But *I'm not finished yet.*

I'LL BE BACK.

And stop looking at me like that. I DON'T LIKE IT.

STATEMENT #1

I'm Louis, George's best friend, and I've been asked to say a few words about him.

The first thing I want to make clear is that I trust George and he's still my mate.

We all thought George was a good guy. A great guy. He was pretty amazing at football. And swimming. Swimming most of all. He was, like, the best in the county. Like a fish.

The thing was, we all thought he was a dude, but he would really get on with the teachers at school as well. Partly because he was clever. But partly because he just didn't do anything nasty. Like, not ever. I don't know how he's got himself into this mess, but I trust him like a brother. I'd trust him with my whole life, man.

Oh yeah. The fire. That shows you what he was like. Jeez, I bet you wouldn't have gone running in there in a thousand years. Not likely that I would have. But he just does it. No crap, straight in, saves a kid's life. That's George. And then he was, like, 'I didn't really think about it – it just sorta happened.' If it was me, I would have been using that on the girls big time, strutting around like a boss. He was still the same old George, though. Exactly as he was before. Funny, nice, top guy.

A million pounds says he's innocent. Ten million. I know this guy, and you don't.

(Do I have to say anything more?)

There was a lot of fuss after the fire.

As well as being in all the papers, I was visited at home by our MP, and patted on the back, *literally*, by the headmistress. There was a special presentation in assembly showing the three fire engines and burnt-out flat. A few people were annoying about it, but most seemed proud that someone from our school had actually done something positive. Girls certainly thought it was impressive. To be honest, I've always been fairly popular with them and have a long-standing girlfriend, Jess. We might, if everything turns out OK, end up being like one of those couples who get together at school and then last forever (she has stuck with me through what has happened – for the record, she's completely and totally amazing).

But you don't need to hear about that, really. I have to explain how I came to go to Australia.

Jess and Louis came with me to the reception at the mayor's house a couple of months after the fire. It was the sort of party that adults moan about beforehand and afterwards but seem to enjoy at the time. All the so-called significant people in Southend were there: councillors, a vicar, important local people . . .

'Ah – here's the hero,' said the mayor. I remember his tanned face shining above his sparkling chain of office. 'I'm honoured to meet you, young man.' I didn't even know Southend had a mayor until all this happened.

'Good evening, Mr Mayor,' I said, remembering my lines, glancing up at Mum and Dad. They were smiling broadly and standing taller than usual. A bit embarrassing, really.

'He's always been such a good boy,' my mum said later in the conversation, making me cringe. 'Even as a baby he didn't really cry.'

After about an hour or so, we all gathered in the main room of the mayor's grand home. Someone tapped a glass and we stopped talking. I remember the mayor's words because they were so *completely* over the top.

'I have been hearing a lot about this young man,' he roared. 'A jolly good egg. He's a brilliant swimmer – one of Southend's, no, one of Essex's, finest – and a great example of a solid local chap.'

I caught Jess's eye. Louis had that slightly open-mouthed, one-eyed-squinting look that usually comes before his funny remarks. He was obviously dying to crack a joke.

'He's also a tremendous football player. But, best of all,' the mayor thundered on, 'he's a very *brave* boy.' The word 'brave' went on so long I thought it would never end. 'A supremely courageous boy. A life-saver.'

Everyone clapped and Jess and Louis whooped and whistled. I wanted to shrivel up.

'I am delighted to announce that George Fleet is also the recipient of a *National Badge of Courage*, of which only four are handed out each year.' The mayor turned to a man on his left. 'And I would like to invite our very special guest, Mr Basil Franklin, to hand out the award.'

Basil Franklin was more important than a mayor. He was something called a *Permanent Secretary* from the government in London. The mayor was even more pleased about Basil Franklin's presence than mine, which was a huge relief.

'Thank you, Mr Mayor,' said Basil Franklin. 'As you say, only four of these awards are handed out each year and, thanks to the munificence of an anonymous donor, they carry material as well as honorific reward.'

The words hazed out. I had no idea what this man was saying. He was too clever to talk to ordinary kids. But soon it was clear even to me that the award brought with it a prize – a big one.

It was that prize which was the second domino on the path to disaster.

I had been given a free place on something called Ultimate Bushcraft. Previous winners had gone on other adventure holidays, mainly to places like the Lake District, or sometimes Spain, I think. But Ultimate Bushcraft was by far the most generous holiday ever to have been awarded. It was a free trip to the north of Australia to experience the outback and do all sorts of outdoor stuff. I can't pretend I didn't think that was incredible. I'd always liked that sort of thing.

'That's unbelievable!' gasped my parents. Turkey was the furthest we'd ever been on holiday.

I was really happy, but I did think at the time that it was a pity that there was only one place. I would have settled for any one of my friends going with me: Louis would have been the obvious choice, but going with Jess would have been great too (though my parents would have been suspicious and her parents, although they're nice, would never have allowed it). But this was for one person only, for just over two weeks, in the summer holidays.

Later, I was pleased the others didn't come because it

would have been *even* worse if anything had happened to them.

I wish I could go back in time and refuse the offer.

'This will be something you'll never forget, young man,' said the mayor.

How right he was.

[Here ends the second part of George's statement]

THE OTHER CHAPTER 2
(SAID IN THE HOUR BEFORE):
HIM

LISTEN.

LISTEN.

LISTEN.

Ultimate Bushcraft. Stupid name. Making something cool by putting the word Ultimate in front of it. And <u>bush</u>craft makes me laugh. *Bush! Get it?*

It was meant to be *character building* for me. *Character building* – what a JOKE!!! My character is like a machine in my chest. It's a machine with wires that go through my body.

The real joke was that *the last straw* was getting caught stealing from a shop the day after I had done someone in. What an absolutely <u>hilarious</u> coincidence.

Not that I had intended to kill Jimmy. That one was just a joke that went a bit too far. I remember him just before he fell, about halfway down the cliff, just before the vertical bit, crapping himself with fear. *Anyone* would have thrown rocks given the situation.

Stop staring. Staring makes me angry.

AS I WAS SAYING, it was the stealing that was *the last*

straw. The laugh-my-arse-off-funny thing is that it was a chicken that I got caught stealing. A chicken. ROFL. ROFL. It was still a mental thing to get caught with up my jumper.

I'm pregnant – that's what I said to the copper who shouldn't have been in the shop anyway. *I'm pregnant*, and then pulled out this chilled chicken. *It's a girl*, I said.

You can laugh.

You should laugh right **now**.

He asked me how it got there. That must be the most stupid question.

It must have flown up there by accident, I said.

Go on – **laugh**.

He made me put the chicken back in the fridge. 'Put it back, son.'

Son? How stupid.

Then he took me home and that's when my grandparents got involved. It was a billion to one chance that they were there.

They wanted me to be part of Ultimate Bushcraft for *character building*. Some bloke at church had told them about it. Typical do-gooders.

Mum didn't care. She just wanted her *medicine*, as she calls it. 'Whatever, whatever . . .' That was her contribution.

Dad thought it should be *beaten* out of me. 'I can knock

some sense into him – he's not too old for that. Three days locked in the small room drinking piss will teach him.'

But Nana and Granddad didn't like the sound of that. 'What he needs is *character* building,' they said. 'Something to bring out his good side. Something to focus on.'

(And did I find *something to focus on*.)

I should just have been left to get on with my life.

But Bushcraft was the least bad thing. It was either that or leave home. And I didn't like the thought of sleeping on the streets.

But that's enough about me.

GEORGEY was there because of that fire crap. What a stupid thing to do – run into a building and rescue some dumb kid and his even dumber mother who should have been barbecued.

But I never told anyone why I was *really* on Ultimate Bushcraft. I made up a stupid story. I just saw the opportunity, being quick when it comes to good opportunities. If I played along nicey-nicey, I could really show them who was BOSS.

<u>And I think you'll agree that's what I did.</u>

STATEMENT #2:

JESSICA MONROE

Hello, my name's Jess, and I'm George's girlfriend. I can't believe what's happened – the George I know wouldn't do those things.

What was he like? He was just . . . George. He was always the same. Always looking out for me, helping me with stuff. Always really calm.

He was really nice with everything. You know what some boys are like, jealous, or trying to get you to do stuff before you're ready, but not George. He's different. He wasn't a wimp, but he didn't try to be all macho.

[Jessica Monroe became upset at this point and there was a pause in the delivery of the statement.]

You've asked me to talk about what he was like before he went on the trip to Australia, and whether he was behaving strangely at all, or whether he mentioned anything to me. He did say that he didn't want to go on his own – I think he probably would have been quite happy not to go at all – but he was positive about it being a really good experience.

The worst thing he ever did? Well, he could be a bit lazy when it came to homework, I suppose, but that's partly because he was really clever, and he sometimes forgot to do stuff. But there was never anything like what you're saying he's done.

I know that he couldn't have had all of that hidden away in his brain. I knew him as well as anyone, probably better than Louis, and I didn't notice anything. He's one of a kind. I'm sure of that. Really, I'm sure. I'm totally sticking by him, and I'd still trust him with my life.

Ultimate Bushcraft was a small company but seemed really well organized. Everyone on the trip was from England, but it was 'crewed' (everything had a special lingo) by Australians – the 'Ozbods', as we were encouraged to call them.

It was an all-boys group: Ultimate Bushcraft ran girls' trips alongside ours, and we'd been promised two or three meetings with the girls, but the 'teams' hiked and did most things separately. The distance from home didn't bother me at all – Southend is only a telephone call away, after all. I was excited, but a bit worried about fitting in (or was I? Maybe that's something I've made up after looking back?).

I was last to arrive at Heathrow. I felt awkward as I walked over – I even wonder whether everything started badly because there was a broken-down lorry on the motorway that made us late. Conversation suddenly stopped and seven boys clambered to their feet. A few of them casually said things like 'Hi' or 'Wassup' or 'G'day', and two tanned men in their early twenties grinned.

'Mate,' said one. 'I'm Jason.' In board shorts, flip-flops and a loud T-shirt, he was like a pantomime Aussie. He wiped his brow and ran his hand through ginger hair. 'Strewth, this is hotter than back home. Meet the rest of the crew.' He waved theatrically at the seven other boys.

Toby seemed to be the senior partner, the reliable one. I sensed Mum and Dad relax as they sized him up. 'G'day,' he said.

'Have a great time, and text us when you have signal,' Mum said.

'And watch out for the Sheilas,' Dad said, winking.

'Now, say bye-bye to Mum and Dad, George,' Jason said.

I gave them both a hug, clumsily, as everyone was watching, and noticed that they held on for slightly longer than usual. They walked away, turning and waving every few paces until the automatic doors to the terminal closed behind them, and they were gone.

'Bye, Mummy; bye, Daddy,' was chimed seven-fold from behind Jason, mockingly. This was clearly the final performance of a custom.

No sooner had they left than my phone rang. It was Jess.

'So you're missing me already,' I whispered, turning away from the group. She said some soppy stuff (which I liked, of course). I mumbled about missing her and looking forward to getting back.

The other guys seemed a bit restless so after about a minute I turned and mouthed *SORRY!*

One second after I'd finished the call, Jason clapped his hands. 'Right, team,' he said. 'Let's go to Oz!'

But my phone was ringing again (Louis, this time) – I again turned away, distracted. I'm pretty sure someone groaned and tutted, but I was distracted by Louis's massively over-the-top spiel about how empty his life was going to be with me away in Australia.

Most of the guys had moved off, but behind me one remaining person spoke. A friendly voice? 'Hey, don't forget your bag.'

'Thanks, I've got it,' I mumbled, not thinking about who I was talking to, in between ending the call with Louis. Then I grabbed my hand-luggage – a rucksack – and dragged my case (weighed that morning to be *exactly* the airline's load limit) haphazardly behind me.

We stood in line while Toby negotiated with a woman in a smart uniform. She then read our names off his list, asking us to present passports and luggage in turn.

Eventually, she said, 'Matthew Lough.'

'Matt,' said the boy I was standing with, glancing at me. 'It's Matt. And it's Luff, not Lock.'

'I'm George,' I said. We hadn't exchanged names, although we'd been chatting.

Matt nodded, as if committing mine to memory while he manoeuvred his case forward. He told me he was on the trip for similar reasons to me: he'd saved a boy who had been trapped on a cliff by climbing up to him, calming him down and calling the police, who'd brought the fire brigade. Matt seemed pretty regular – a normal kid who'd somehow got caught up in something extraordinary without really realizing it. Just like me.

Next it was my turn.

'Can I see your passport, love?' and, 'Did you pack your own bag?' and, 'Can you plonk that on the machine?' all passed in a blur.

'Don't strain yourself,' muttered a boy with a deep voice a few feet behind as I heaved the case on to the conveyor belt.

Toby frowned at him. 'Thank you, Nick. George doesn't need your input.' He gave me a smile that suggested we were on the same side.

Nick breathed out deeply and stared ahead, his narrow

eyes unblinking. He was tall with wiry brown hair and wore a plain black T-shirt and jeans.

I was chatting to Matt again as we arrived at Security. Toby gave the lot of us a pretty firm talk about being sensible and doing exactly what we were told.

To avoid trouble, I placed everything that could possibly set off the scanner into the tray. Everything from my pockets, as well as my belt, shoes, even a bit of tissue from my back pocket that had apparently been through the washing machine. But I still glanced at the archway as I went through to check that the light was green.

Almost immediately the X-ray machine next to me flashed red and two or three extra security people stepped forward.

'Is the blue rucksack yours?' a woman said to Matt, holding the offending bag at arm's length like a rotting fish. I knew it wasn't. Matt's was plastered in Arsenal red. 'Blue with a Southend United badge?'

'It's mine,' I stammered, feeling my face redden as Toby dashed back to see what the problem was.

'Please step to one side,' said the woman to me. She then turned aggressively to Toby. 'Are you the boy's father?' It was a daft thing to say. Toby didn't look remotely old enough to be my father. 'Brother?' she snapped.

'I'm responsible for the boy on a residential trip,' Toby said calmly.

The woman's finger (I remember there being a long blue fingernail on the end of it) beckoned Toby to the side of the machine where the X-ray display was, and then tapped the screen.

'What have I done?' I asked, blood draining from my face.

'Why don't you come and see what we can see?' said the woman, guiding me by the arm round to the screen. People muttered in the lengthening queue behind me.

There was no doubt what was in my bag. I could see the barrel and trigger and . . . A perfect gun shape. 'It's wrapped in something,' she said.

'But there can't be a gun in my bag,' I spluttered.

'Young man, that's obviously not just a bottle of water, is it?' said a man's voice. He had SUPERVISOR written on a badge on his chest.

'But – I don't even *own* a gun.'

'Then who does this belong to?' the woman asked, plucking out a plastic toy gun that was wrapped up inside a piece of paper. The woman straightened out the paper on the desk. It was a ripped-out magazine page with a picture of a woman, probably from a lad's mag. (I was actually relieved it wasn't something worse from the internet.) In other circumstances I would have laughed. But my hands went to my mouth and I shook my head and turned away. 'I promise you that this has got nothing to do with me . . .'

[Here ends the third part of George's statement]

THE OTHER CHAPTER 3
(SAID IN THE HOUR BEFORE):
HIM

You kept us waiting. Did you walk in late on purpose to make an entrance? *Of course you did.*

I knew from that first moment that Georgey would be SOFT. Full of wind and puff, mushy like a slug. Blond hair like a girl's.

Glutinous George. *Gummy* George. *Gooey* George.

All that answering of telephones and poncy talk with some girl – I felt hatred stir right THEN.

Pompous and proud – one hundred per cent full of himself.

Full of shite as well. So far up his own arse that he could do the ultimate disappearing act and climb right up there.

There are so many things that are more worthwhile than you: gerbils, gnats, a plectrum.

Did you like that? HA! And if you don't bloody well laugh I'll hit you again. YOU REALLY AREN'T LEARNING, ARE YOU? I've told you before. Don't. Make. Me. Tell. You. Again.

And earwax. I meant to say earwax.

The others had character, but you're just fluff, Georgey. Bum fluff.

Did you like that? Bum fluff. HA!

True, true, there is one thing I can say. I could see PRINCIPLES. All hail Georgey and his bloody big principles. Big enough to soak up sick. Which is what they made me. You understand what I'm saying? Georgey is an arsehole.

Now, you might be thinking that I'm not your *average guy*.

Don't shake your head – I know that's what you're thinking.

But it's MUCH more complicated than that. You see, and let's get this straight right now, I'm HONEST. That's the difference between YOU and ME.

Now stay with me on this. I'll speak very quietly and very slowly so that you can un-DERRRR-stand.

And stop bleeding while I talk to you.

Where was I?

Yes.

HONEST. I'm honest.

One – when I hate someone, I just admit right away that I hate them. I don't pretend it's a medieval crusade and justify it for some other made-up reason. Some people just get on my tits. I'm happy admitting that. Usually, I'd like to kill them. Or at least make them go away and suffer.

Two – I do what I enjoy. *Do what thou wilt shall be the whole of the Law*. You're too thick to understand. It means

33

you should just do whatever the hell you like. Most people do. I just take it to – <u>listen</u> to these words – *a logical extreme*. <u>You take everything to its logical extreme</u>, a teacher once said. I certainly took things to a logical extreme with her. The evil cow.

And **three**. Listen to this one. You'll love it. It's the most ball-breakingly <u>HONEST</u> thing you'll ever have heard. I sometimes get jealous.

I bet you've never <u>ever</u> admitted that.

And that brings me to *Georgey*. Strutting in, hair smelling of some fancy shampoo, straight from the gym, stuffed full of vitamins, all dressed in cotton. Blue-eyed boy. People would <u>think</u> Georgey was perfect.

That made him a LIAR.

I'm the one who is perfectly honest. **I'm** the <u>perfect</u> decision-maker. Look into my eyes and tell me that I'm not a KING.

Anyway, I need to finish my part of the story.

So, you kept us all waiting. Everyone had been talking to me, and we were getting on very nicely. I was doing my funny accent and making everyone laugh.

And then they all turned to Georgey. I **hated** them for that, and had an idea of revenge even then. You warbled on in that ridiculously posh voice.

There was no doubt whose bag I would put the toy gun in.

'Don't forget your bag,' I said, immediately after I slipped the thing into the outer pocket. Remember? It was a joke, but everyone was too thick to see it. Totally <u>hilarious</u>.

I amaze myself. I'm the **KING** of the world with **power** over life and death.

(Oh yeah – the disgusting picture I wrapped the toy gun in? Clever, eh?)

STATEMENT #3

NATHANIEL BAILEY

My name is Mr Nathaniel Bailey, and I was George Fleet's form tutor at St William's High School in Southend. I've known George for three years.

He was conscientious and did very well in his GCSEs, and had made a good start to his A levels; he probably would have gone on to a decent university, though he was even better known as a sportsman: his swimming was brilliant and he represented St William's for football and athletics.

George appeared helpful. If you had asked me a couple of weeks ago, I would have said he was a model pupil. But with so many students to look after, it is difficult to know any one child as well as one might hope.

George had a broad group of friends. I now wonder if they were rather reliant on him. Perhaps, thinking about it, he might have been too much a leader of the group rather than a member of it. Louis, who I think you've spoken to, worshipped George, and did sometimes get into trouble. It could be that George was behind that. I don't know.

The last report I wrote for George was very positive, but we are asked to be as positive as possible.

To summarize, we didn't have a problem with George, but children are complicated sometimes, and teachers can only report what they see.

Thank you.

CHAPTER 4
(LATER ON IN THE NINTH DAY BEFORE):
THE FOURTH PART OF GEORGE'S STATEMENT

You know when you meet someone and you're sure that you're going to get on with them? That's how I felt about Matt. 'A babe in a swimsuit!' he laughed. 'How old are you? Twelve?' He loudly, though not entirely seriously, pleaded my case to the security people. 'Can't you see that this nice young man is innocent when it comes to such things?' he joked. I didn't know whether to act naive or tell Matt to shut up.

'None of it's mine,' I mumbled.

Toby was great. He half implied that it was all my stupid fault, but half suggested that it was an irresponsible prank played on me. I don't think they quite knew which one to believe. My apologies finally seemed to win them over. The gun was clearly a plastic toy one – the sort that fires foam pellets. It was orange and blue. Fortunately, the supervisor seemed like a nice guy who saw the funny side.

As we walked away, Toby said to me, 'I don't think we'll have any more of that, OK, mate?'

I knew that arguing about it would get me nowhere, and might even suggest that I was guilty, so I said that I 'would be more careful in future'. That hinted to Toby that I had learned my lesson, but meant I didn't *actually* lie and admit to more guilt that I really had. And I *would* be careful – because someone had put that toy gun in my bag on purpose, deliberately trying to get me in trouble. But it had come out of the blue. I had always got on with people before.

Matt had a peculiar look in his eye, perhaps wondering if the toy gun really was mine.

'For a moment, I thought it was curtains,' I said. 'I just can't work it out.'

'You know – I *actually* believe you,' said Matt. 'You were calm, man. I would have gone totally mad if that was found in my bag. I would have been as mad as a bee. As mad as a bee with a bee up its bum.'

I laughed and knew we were friends. I want to write *friends to the end*, but that just makes me feel bad.

There were three of us, though, who went around the shops on the far side of security. Almost straight after the gun-and-picture incident, Nick walked up to us and introduced himself. 'I think we're sitting together on the plane,' he said in his very deep voice. 'According to Jason,

I'm 41H, and you two are 41J and K.' For some reason, the team wasn't in one row on the plane, but separated into two threes and a four. Nick looked a bit older than the rest of us – like he could grow a beard if he wanted to. He was a big guy, but there was no fat on him – I'm a fairly good athlete, but I wouldn't have wanted to race him.

There isn't a massive amount more to tell you about Heathrow. There were no clues as to what was going to happen, though I've been through it a million times in my mind. Toby gathered us all together and made us leave our bags in a pile next to him before we went off round the shops. After a brief talk about not getting into trouble *again*, he nodded at Matt, and said to everyone: 'And no nuts, remember.'

We had been warned about this before we left for the airport, and Mum had methodically been through my bag removing Snickers and Peanut M&Ms. Matt, apparently, had a nut allergy.

'I haven't had any problems for a couple of years,' Matt said defensively, palms up. 'Stay calm, people.'

I stocked up with as many cans of Coke and bags of nut-less sweets as I could reasonably carry. It was a long flight, after all.

Matt was with me throughout, chattering away about nothing much, telling jokes, putting on funny accents.

Nick was harder to decipher. He threw in the occasional quip or cynical aside. I wondered if he had more to say but chose not to share it.

It was when we were airborne and well on our way to Singapore that something important happened.

Everyone was getting on just fine, I thought. I didn't know the other boys well at that stage, but was sitting in the middle of a trio of seats with Matt (next to the window) and Nick (next to the aisle, fortunately, as he was really tall), all of us on electronic devices of one sort or another. Airline food had come round, but was left untouched apart from the drink; it didn't look too bad, but couldn't compare with thousands of sweets and crisps.

'If I eat another Pringle, I'll do a Mr Creosote,' Matt said, before popping another crisp in his mouth and farting. Mr Creosote was, he said, a bloke in a film who exploded from eating too much.

A warning had gone out over the tannoy about Matt's nut allergy. By chance, there were two other people on the flight with the same problem, so the captain explained that no one should even open a packets of nuts, instead 'they could have some in the transfer lounge at Singapore'.

Sitting next to Matt, aware of the amount of sharing of sweets going on, I vaguely kept an eye out for nut-infested things, but saw nothing.

Another packet of Haribos had been slowly passed around. The plane was making a low hum as it came in closer to Singapore, and we had all quietened down, ready for descent. My head was just beginning to feel heavy when Matt nudged me.

'Can you help me find my inhaler?' He was patting his pockets and looking a bit flustered.

'Where do you keep it?' I asked.

'Normally-it's-in-my-bag,' he panted.

I dragged his bag up from under the seat and rooted around in the largest section. It was packed with things for the journey, books and magazines and stuff, but no inhaler.

Matt was soon clutching his chest and his lips were swollen and red. A sort of speckled rash was on his cheeks.

Nick was on my left. 'Get Toby!' I said. 'Right now.'

Ever more frantically, I searched in the zipped front section of the rucksack, and there, underneath a yellow pen-like device that I recognized from school, was an inhaler.

Matt took two puffs immediately, but it was no use. He couldn't get enough of the stuff in.

'Toby's not in his seat. I think he might be having a piss,' said Nick.

'Then get someone else – right now!' I said.

It all happened so quickly. Matt was beginning to droop. He was holding his side and his eyes were widening and narrowing. He couldn't breathe properly. 'I-need . . .' He was pointing at the EpiPen.

'Can you get him out from his seat? That'll help,' said a man from the row in front.

'Hey! Can someone help? Is there a doctor?' said a woman from behind who'd noticed the commotion. 'Can someone do something?'

This time was different to the fire. This wasn't a big distant problem that I was drawn towards – it was a horror right next to me. Suddenly panic was flapping around and Jason appeared, saying, 'What do you think the problem is? What should we do?'

It was obvious what had happened: one way or another, Matt had eaten something that contained nuts and was in serious trouble. I didn't say anything, even when I vaguely heard the flight attendant asking me to move. Do things step by step, I thought to myself.

'Is there a doctor on the plane?' came over the tannoy, more than once, an urgent – no, *panicked* – voice.

I snapped the top off the EpiPen, pulled it back a bit from Matt's leg, and then – just as the picture showed – plunged it down into Matt's thigh. It said to leave it there for ten seconds.

I counted out the ten seconds. To be honest, I was surprised at how easily it went through his jeans. People were still talking and shouting for the first three or four, but by the time I reached seven the only thing that could be heard was my voice.

When I was between eight and nine, though, Matt whispered, 'Thanks.'

'Nine . . . ten,' I finished. 'Now we need to lie him down across the seats.'

I pulled out the device and clambered out into the aisle. Two flight attendants, with Toby looking on, put up the seat arms and laid Matt down.

The injection had helped Matt almost straight away. His breathing was weak, but steady. He angled his head round towards me and said, 'Thanks, mate.'

'That was bloody amazing,' said Jason. A few people clapped. Nearly all of the group clustered round us, talking.

I also heard, 'That was great to see.' At the time, I thought it was a compliment about the way I'd handled things. But now I'm not so sure.

[Here ends the fourth part of George's statement]

THE OTHER CHAPTER 4
(SAID IN THE HOUR BEFORE):
HIM

Matt had nuts. Then he went nuts. Get it?

I can see you're wondering <u>how</u> I did it.

I can see you're wondering <u>why</u> I did it.

For a start, I thought he was a **FAKER**.

And I couldn't believe the reason why he was on the trip. What a numbskull. He went up a cliff to save some kid when he could have got him down a lot faster by throwing a few stones at him! All you need is one stone to hit him right there on the head and he'd have fallen like a tenpin.

SPLAT!

Having him and me on the same trip is called *irony*.

AND, he was falling over himself with love for Georgey. Probably wanted to have your kids.

I didn't buy the peanuts in the airport, anyway. I brought them along before – packed them when the warnings were given out. NO – it wasn't exactly a PLAN. But I thought I'd have them just in case. Just in case I wanted to do an experiment on the **FAKER**.

I did it all to <u>perfection</u>. I went to the toilet and opened up the two packets. It was like a scientific investigation. I crushed up the peanuts very small, little more than dust. I tell you, that was the most exciting bit of all. Then I sprinkled some on to the sweets.

Tasty.

I AM THE MASTER. I COMMAND LIFE AND DEATH.

You need to remember that. Just one little <u>twist</u> and you'll join the others.

I slid the packet along the row of four. 'Oh, whose sweets are they?' I asked about half an hour later. 'Do you mind if I have one?' then – ever so innocently – 'Shall we pass them round?'

So generous, you see.

What I STILL don't understand is why so much fuss was made over a little bit of wheezing and a stab in the leg with that machine.

I mean, it was all *highly* entertaining, better than TV, but anyone could have rammed that pen thing into his leg. It just had to be *you*. So keen to take all the credit – you didn't even let the stewardess help. Selfish bastard.

The absolute top thing is that no one suspected I did it. Some bloke at the back got the blame for opening a packet of cashews. HILARIOUS!

My sides might split with laughter and all my guts fall out.

I'm getting bored with this. I think we might play a game.

RECONSTRUCTED FOR PURPOSES OF THIS STATEMENT #4

MATTHEW (MATT) LOUGH

SINGAPORE, before leaving for Sydney and then Cairns. Matt Lough, after his anaphylactic shock:

'Mum, can I talk now, please? Let me say something. Like, can I speak? [Silence on the line.] So, I must have eaten something. This geezer at the back, the prat, had some cashews out, and I had gone past to the bogs, and you know it was cashews last time. [Silence on the line.] Are you still there? Earth to mother? Alien visitor calling mother ship? Come in, come in.

['Yes. I'm here.']

So, George, who's with us because he also did something heroic in a fire, was like cool as a cucumber and stabbed me with the EpiPen. By then we were thirty minutes from Singapore, so we came here anyway. And now I'm fine. Absolutely fine. No need to be in hospital at all. Ready to go to Oz. *Comprendo?*'

[Matt's mother expresses disagreement.]

'Are you kidding me? What's the point of that? The time I needed you was when I was at 35,000 feet and

48

couldn't breathe. Look, I'm fine – listen. [Matt breathes clearly down the line.] If you agree, I can go on and join the party. Why do you want to punish me? Coming back home would be stupid. You coming here would be even stupider. Me going to Oz and having a sick time would be A star.'

[Matt's mother is slowly being won round.]

'I know that Dad agrees with me. I can hear him thinking: good boy, Matt son, you go on to Oz and impress the girls with your muscular muscles.'

[This argument helps only very slightly.]

'I'll just be slightly late. Come on, Mum, you know it makes sense!'

CHAPTER 5
(EIGHT DAYS BEFORE):
THE FIFTH PART OF
GEORGE'S STATEMENT

With Matt getting better by the minute and the quick thinking of Toby and the Ultimate Bushcraft people in Australia, the trip wasn't cancelled, so we continued on to Sydney with only a tiny delay. Later came the good news that Matt would rejoin us fairly soon.

The seating was rearranged on the second leg of the journey – probably a good thing, because I hadn't really been able to make a connection with Nick. I was put in another row of three, this time between Lee and Luke. Both were real individuals.

I suppose it's simplest to say that Lee was a nerd. At first, I wondered if it was shyness (it wasn't). He had some unusual facts that I found interesting, but wouldn't have thought to share if I'd known them. 'Did you know that Boeing is named after a man called William E. Boeing?' and 'QANTAS is a really unusual word because it doesn't have a U after the Q, and that's because it is an acronym', for example. But there was something darker about him: 'If we crashed, how long do you think it would hurt for?

Would it hurt a lot for a fraction of a second? I think so. Would it hurt more than the knowledge that you were about to die?' Matt's allergic reaction was taboo for the rest of us, but Lee did mention it, almost as if thinking aloud: 'I wonder if he thought he was going to die. I wonder what that felt like.'

I kept on pulling the subject back to everyday things, wondering what was below us out of the window, or suggesting that we had a bit of sleep. I really tried to be nice.

Luke was – how can I put this – *not* going to be a rugby player. He was slim and perfectly dressed in a button-down shirt and a really smart dark red jersey. His voice was a bit high-pitched and he used his hands a lot when he was speaking. He couldn't seem to sit still.

I remember one conversation in particular.

'Oh my God,' he said, waking me up. 'I'm so sorry.' Luke had spilt some water and some of it had gone on my shirt and trousers. 'Do you want a tissue?'

'That's OK,' I said sleepily. 'It's only water. It'll soon dry.'

'I'm really sorry. I'm just all thumbs when I get tired.'

'That's OK, Luke.' I gave him a friendly nudge, just to

let him know I didn't mind, then settled back into my seat and shut my eyes.

'Thanks. Thanks, Georgey,' were the last words I heard as I drifted off to sleep.

Georgey – it was the first time I had ever been called that.

I was blotto as we flew over a chunk of Asia and most of Australia, then the reminder to put your seatbelt on woke me up. Jason and Nick were in the aisle, returning to their seats.

'Welcome to the mother country, mate,' said Jason.

'Put on your seat belt – like a good boy,' added Nick.

Luke was in my ear as well: 'It's so exciting. We're here, Georgey, we're here!'

Sydney was hidden by thick cloud until just before we landed. As rain hammered down on the metal and glass of the airport roof, Jason said, 'The weather's been put on to make you boys feel at home.' There were quite a few jokes about other things we thought we knew about Australia not being true: 'And are we going to find out that you don't play cricket here?' and 'I suppose you don't drink beer and never have barbecues?'

Sydney airport was big and felt like another Heathrow.

We were all tired after the journey and I had that heavy cotton-wool feeling in my head, so was on autopilot most of the time.

I have to mention one thing that happened in Sydney airport because of the CCTV footage. I can remember exactly what happened, though it sounds stupid and really childish.

I wanted to sit on my case and shut my eyes, but Luke kept on telling me stupid jokes to keep me awake. It was all light-hearted. You can see Luke laughing on the film. I only pretended to shoot him to shut him up – it was all part of the joke. I can't see why there's been so much fuss over it.

Jason then appears on the CCTV footage. I realize that this bit looks bad, but I was really tired and, I suppose, trying to make the others laugh. The background is that we had been told about why the girls' group didn't travel with us from London – Toby had said that there was a mess-up with the booking, so we had gone with QANTAS rather than British Airways, but that we might rendezvous in Sydney.

Just as I had sat down on my case, Jason (with a tall, thin boy with black hair called Peter) appeared to explain that the slight delay because of Matt meant that rendezvous wouldn't happen.

(With his back to the camera) Jason said, 'Guys, there won't be any girls until we get to Cairns. Their flight has already gone.'

'That's a shame,' said Luke, jigging around. 'I'll just have to put up with Georgey's company.'

It was at that point I closed my eyes. 'Thanks, *mate*,' I said to Jason.

Jason then said to Luke, presumably because my eyes were closed: 'I don't think George is listening to me, so you can make sure he gets the message.'

When I opened my eyes and saw Jason and Peter walking away, I stood up and gestured one shooting motion towards Jason. It was all in the context of having done the same to Luke.

It was stupid but innocent. I'm not perfect.

Anyway, I wouldn't even have mentioned it except so much time has been wasted on it already.

On the final three-hour flight to Cairns I was in the very back row next to Toby. It didn't feel awkward in the way that it would sitting next to a teacher. Jason and Peter were across the aisle and they were deep in conversation much of the time.

Toby was the sort of guy I looked up to: really nice

54

and often funny; cool (without trying) and in control. He seemed to like me. Jason sometimes spoke to Toby, and I caught snatches of their conversation between sleeps. First, Jason was talking about how he came to be a leader on the trip – he had volunteered because he wanted to do something fun and helpful rather than live an empty life making money. I heard Toby explaining he was doing Ultimate Bushcraft in a gap year after finishing at university, then he hoped to be a teacher, maybe in England. He'd been travelling around Europe with his girlfriend for a few weeks before meeting us in Heathrow and thought London was pretty cool.

Toby and Jason; Luke, Lee, Peter, and the others – I stupidly thought they'd wander in and out of my life leaving only happy memories.

I couldn't have been more wrong.

[Here ends the fifth part of George's statement]

Even tyrants must sleep. That's the saying.

And I saw you sleep. Sleep through the bit of turbulence, sleep through that **STUPID** woman complaining about us. I could have done anything and you would have been powerless to stop me. I could have tied your laces together. I could have put a beetle in your ear. I could have *shot* you.

SAY that I make you laugh. Go on. SAY IT. SAY IT NOW.

You were talking to that *really* strange one sitting next to you, smarming up to him, brown-nosing so that everyone would love *Georgey*.

I'll admit – with honesty, more honesty than YOU have, *remember* – that I was a little bit jealous.

And it was then that my hatred began to grow. Like a beanstalk.

Now, I said that I would tell you something about ME.

Let's start with Mummy and Daddy. Sometimes a man and a woman don't love one another very much and they produce a baby.

Mummy. She's a cardboard cut-out. Like the ones you

see in the cinema when there's a big film showing. Easily knocked over. All make-up and smiles. And Valium.

And Daddy. He's the man on the moon. The ogre at the top of the beanstalk.

I was always totally different to them. I would read and think and experiment, and they would watch TV and shout and then make up in the sitting room.

They hated me from the start. It's a surprise I've turned out *SO* normal.

Oh yeah. I'll answer the question you've been dying – <u>dying</u>, get it? – to ask. When did I decide to start my master plan?

It was after what happened when we arrived in Cairns.

I had to get **REVENGE**.

STATEMENT #5

VALERIE COLLINS

Mrs Valerie Collins was on the same flight that the Ultimate Bushcraft group took from Singapore to Sydney:

Yes. I remember those boys sitting in the row behind us. I have to say they made a horrid racket, fuelled by an awful amount of sugar no doubt. They really should have been better controlled. I did complain. They were continually going up and down the aisles, to the loo, passing sweets to one another, throwing fizzy pop around. And the one you described, George Fleet, I *think* I can remember him. He was a brooding presence in the background, I suppose, as much as I can recall.

CHAPTER 6
(ONE WEEK BEFORE):
THE SIXTH PART OF
GEORGE'S STATEMENT

Sydney may have been in their 'winter', but Cairns, in Queensland at the top of Australia, is pretty much always summer – wet summer at Christmas, and dry summer in July. It was cloudy, but the heat hit us the moment we stepped outside, lugging our bags after us, saying nothing.

We threw ourselves on to a minibus that was driven by a girl called Andrea. She was probably four or five years older than us, and had light brown hair and was pretty and tanned. We all raised our eyebrows and muttered comments, at least until she and Toby had a kiss that showed they were more than just friends . . .

'I missed you on the journey,' I heard her say to him.

On the minibus, I happened to end up sitting next to Peter. Peter Emsworth-Lyle. I'd hardly spoken to him so far. The first five minutes were spent admiring his new red-and-black Emporio Armani trainers. His voice was posh – more than posh, it was sneering. He didn't waste any time telling me that his dad was a top banker and his mum a top lawyer. His parents had paid for the trip so that they could tour Europe without leaving him at home alone in Chelsea.

The story sounded a bit weird, but possibly only because I didn't live in the world of yachts and five-star hotels.

'Do you mind being away from them?' I asked.

'They've always been in another dimension,' he said. 'I don't get on with either of them. That's why they sent me to boarding school in Scotland when I was seven. They try and make themselves feel better by buying me expensive stuff – like these trainers. Though I doubt *you* know much about designer clothes.'

I knew it was an insult but let it go. 'So being away from home is normal to you, then?'

'*Everything* is pretty normal to me, George. *Absolutely* everything.'

It wasn't only the conversation that was difficult. I remember now how the journey was made uncomfortable because the knees of the boy behind were sticking in my back. It wasn't exactly his fault – the wheel arch made it difficult for him to fit in.

Reg kept on apologizing. 'Sorry, George, I'm very sorry . . . I can't keep my knees out the way. Sorry, George, I really didn't want to do that . . . There's not enough room.' After Peter and I had stopped talking, microsleeps

were interrupted with, 'Sorry, George. Sorry, George . . .'
The apologies, to be honest, were more annoying than
the knees. Reg stood out in the group because he was big
(by which I mean fat), probably 18 stone, maybe more. I
mention it because the story of that first night in Australia
is mainly about Reg.

We arrived in the late afternoon, about two hours after
leaving Cairns Airport, but it could have been a million
miles away.

'Welcome to Thorpe Cove,' said Toby. *Thorpe Cove* –
the words make me shudder now, but at the time it was
exciting. It was a smallish bay with a perfect sandy beach
with trees on either side dipping down into the water. The
sun was sinking behind the hills beyond the house. Five
canoes had been dragged high on to the golden sand. We
stood and swore in admiration. For a short time, we really
were one unit.

'This is where you'll be based for the first four days,
guys. Satisfied?' said Toby.

We all nodded and smiled.

'Not bad, eh?' said Jason.

Toby was very much in charge. 'After you've all had
a shower, I'll explain what we're going to do. Don't
hang around.'

The accommodation was basic but clean, a bit like the sort of thing you get on a school trip, but with two people sharing rooms that could sleep eight, each with a small toilet attached. There was one big shower room with ten cubicles and a large open area with about six shower heads.

I had a room to myself, at least until Matt caught up with us. The others were sharing. This was Toby's decision. He said it wasn't a *reward* for what happened on the plane, but because he thought Matt would like it.

I dumped my stuff immediately and dashed to the shower to avoid the crowd that was bound to follow. In fact, without the delay of having someone else in my room to talk to, I was washed and out before the next person arrived. It was Nick, the guy who had been sitting next to me on the plane when Matt had his attack.

'All right, George,' he said, catching my eye for a second and then openly scrutinizing my chest. 'I see you've been down the gym.'

'I'm a bit of a swimmer and do land training every now and again.' I knew that was an understatement, but didn't want to boast. 'But I'm never going to win the Olympics.' I had a quick glance at Nick, who was also just in a towel. I knew I was pretty trim, but he was a block of proper muscle. Immediately after my glance, he dropped his towel and stood there with nothing on. I made sure that I kept looking straight into his eyes.

Lee and Luke (who were sharing a room) entered at that point, chatting away, ignoring Nick and me.

'I've got some protein supplements and some other stuff if you're interested,' Nick said quietly. 'Not things you can get on the open market.'

Looking at Lee and Luke rather than at Nick, I tried to explain that I was interested in swimming rather than body building. Given that he was definitely into the latter, I didn't want to insult him.

'Don't try to be perfect all the time,' he said, a hint of ice creeping into his voice for the first time. 'Nobody wants that.'

'I'll let you know,' I said cagily, making for the door without turning round as two others then came in, which meant everyone was there apart from Reg. Just for a second I wondered if Reg had delayed his arrival because at least some undressing had to happen in the central part of the shower room in front of everyone.

'Yeah. Let me know, mate,' said Nick, now behind his shower curtain.

Jason, just in trunks, was leaning on the open door into

Reg's room when I passed by on the way back to my room. He was encouraging Reg into the shower room. 'Come on, mate, you'll need plenty of time to wash.' There was a bit of a chuckle in his voice.

I wasn't sure whether this was a joke about Reg's size. I poked my head round his door. 'See you outside afterwards,' I said.

'Do you want to take over?' Jason said straight away. 'I can see you're in charge.'

I felt embarrassed. 'See you in a bit, Reg,' I said, and then to Jason: 'Sorry.'

'Yeah, yeah,' Jason said, walking away, stretching his arms out as if doing front crawl. 'I think I'll go and wash in the sea.'

Feeling a bit bruised by these conversations with both Nick and Jason, and (to be really honest) probably a bit irritated by lack of sleep, I went into my room and tried to get the Wi-Fi to work on my iPad so that I could Skype Jess and Louis (and Mum and Dad). My room looked out on to the bay and in the distance I could just about see Jason in the water – he looked like he could be a good swimmer if he had a bit of training.

Maybe twenty minutes later, Alastair, who everyone called Al, put his head round my door. He and I had only said a few words to one another up to this point, but he seemed friendly enough. 'Time to meet on the beach,' he said. 'Oh – did you get Wi-Fi?'

I explained that I could only get a very slight signal on the iPad and one blob on my phone.

'Maybe we can try together after the talk?' Al suggested.

We walked outside to the beach. Toby was sitting on one of three long logs that were laid out to make a triangle; Peter and Nick were whispering together on another and glancing back at the building, while Luke and Lee sat on the third – so they were in room formation. Alastair and I made six. Only Reg and Jason were missing.

I had just sat down next to Toby when Jason ran out of the building, barefoot and still damp from his swim, and parked himself next to Peter.

'What's keeping Reg?' asked Nick. 'Is he still drying himself? It'd be a major operation.'

There was some laughter, but not from me, partly because Toby didn't laugh.

'What *is* keeping him?' Toby said. 'George, could you run and have a look?'

(I am sure he asked me because I was next to him, rather than out of favouritism.)

I'd only gone a couple of paces when Reg appeared at

the door to the house, which was about a hundred yards away. He wasn't wearing anything but was holding (I found out later) one of Alastair's shirts in front of him to avoid being completely naked. He was shouting and agitated. There was a fair bit of swearing as well, which I'll miss out: 'Where've you put my clothes?' he yelled, seemingly at all of us. 'And my towel and everything? Where are they?' He was almost crying with frustration.

Toby started running towards him and I followed. I could hear Peter and Nick hooting with laughter and I fired an angry stare at them. Looking back, I realize I looked like a stupid do-gooder. But I didn't stay out of it, and that's that.

'I'll kill whoever's done this!' Reg snarled at me. Then to the others: 'I hate you all!'

'You can put some of my clothes on,' I offered stupidly. 'Come on, Reg, let's go inside.'

'I can't fit into your clothes, you thick bastard,' he shouted at me.

'Reg, I think you should . . .' Toby started.

'You let this happen,' Reg shouted at Toby.

'Reg, I want us to be friends,' I said pretty firmly. 'But you need to calm down, mate.'

My words had an immediate effect. Reg's voice

lightened. Transformed. 'Then please find my clothes. Rather than just standing there looking at my sexy body . . .' He turned, bum on full view to the other boys, which set Nick and Peter off again, and went inside, followed by Toby.

I was going to follow, but sudden anger messed with my judgement. The idea of someone bullying this boy – and bullying is what this was – burnt within me. (Why? OK – it's because I slightly bullied someone at school years ago and have felt guilty about it ever since. You can investigate that if you like, and may want to use it against me, but it was about six years ago and has really made me stand up for anyone who is bullied ever since.) I strode back to the others.

'Where the hell have you put his stuff?' I said to Peter and Nick.

'That was bloody funny, but I didn't do it,' drawled Peter, who was as thin as Reg was fat, but no one thought to laugh at that. 'And don't speak to *me* like that. I'm not your slave.'

'Not me, guv,' shrugged Nick, sneering, but then more serious. 'Not after a fight, are you? Coming over here and lording it over us.'

Jason, still sitting next to Peter, was silent.

'I don't *want* to fight,' I said. For a couple of seconds I revved like a car in neutral, then decided to take a different tack. 'Look, why don't we all look for his stuff? Then the person, or *people*, who've hidden it can find it for Reg.'

'Sounds like a good plan,' said Lee. 'It's logical to start inside the house.'

Luke said he'd check outside, round the back.

'Come on then boys *and girls*.' Finally, Jason had spoken. The *girls*, judging by his stare, were Lee, Luke and me.

Everyone scattered. Peter and Nick wandered aimlessly around the front of the house, looking half-heartedly, possibly because they felt falsely accused, or probably, I thought, because if they headed straight to the hiding place they'd look properly guilty.

Luke and Alastair appeared to take the search seriously. I glanced out of one of the back windows of the house and saw them moving methodically around the car park and surrounding vegetation. Alastair lay on his side and checked under the minibus.

Lee and I then met in the middle of the house, having searched from opposite ends. We could hear a much calmer Reg talking to Toby and Jason inside his room.

'What would Sherlock Holmes do?' asked Lee.

I said that I didn't have any idea, and wasn't sure how logical or intelligent someone who stole all a boy's clothes would be.

'But someone like that would think logically according to their own internal rationality.'

'OK,' I said, playing along. 'They'd either destroy the clothes completely . . .'

Lee put up his hands, pausing slightly while preparing something clever to say. 'There's no fire without smoke. I see no evidence of total destruction.'

'Right,' I said, shrugging. 'So, well, I'd do something dumb with them. I don't know – float them out to sea?'

'Good thinking. And how would you do that?'

'Put them in a canoe?' I wondered.

'Exactly,' said Lee. 'Are you sure you're not responsible? But there were five canoes when we first arrived and there are still five now. I thought of that.'

'I'm guessing *you're* not responsible.' I chuckled.

'Perhaps I am,' said Lee, 'and this conversation is a clever way for me to cover my highly intelligent tracks. But proceeding on the premise that I'm not the wrongdoer, and assuming that the culprit didn't do anything destructive, he'd want to do something annoying . . .' He sighed.

'Hold on, Lee,' I said. 'You *are* a genius. And he wouldn't have long to act – where does the rubbish go?'

Lee pointed to the door at the far end of the passageway. 'Out there, I think.'

As we left the house, and turned to the fenced-off area that looked as if it held the wheelie bins, Luke was just returning from his car-park search. 'I've already looked in there,' he shouted. 'Nothing. Full of rubbish. It stinks!'

I went in anyway, with Lee and Luke following.

'I see what you mean,' I said as I opened the first bin. The second was only half full. The third had a black sack on top – but when I nudged it with my finger, more of a prod than a proper investigation, I realized it was an empty one stretched over the top of a silver suitcase.

'Elementary, my dear George,' said Lee.

'Well done, Superhero Georgey,' said Luke.

From outside came Peter's drawling voice: 'Found any rubbish in there?'

'We've found this,' I said triumphantly, pulling out the case with Luke's reluctant help.

'He who smelt it dealt it, that's what I think,' said Nick. 'So you know who I think hid it: he who went straight to where it was hidden.'

'Come on, man,' Alastair, who had wandered over from the minibus, said. 'We all know George didn't do it.'

'I'm getting this back to Reg,' I said, rolling the case towards the door. I was pretty sure Nick and Peter were responsible – it seemed obvious – so it was with a look at them that I said, 'Let's hope that's the last bit of *bullying*.' It must have sounded a bit pompous, but I wanted to take a stand.

'Get over yourself, George Fleet,' Nick shot back angrily. 'What a prick!'

I think things would have turned nasty if Jason hadn't opened the door right then. 'Jeez, well done, team!' he said, apparently oblivious to the tension.

It took about half an hour for us all, Reg included, to assemble on the logs, by which time it was beginning to get dark. It was still very hot, though, and some of the group were only wearing shorts. That was how I noticed Alastair's scar.

While we ate curry, Toby gave us a lecture about the need to work together – and that Ultimate Bushcraft could only be a success if we worked as a team. He did the usual thing of asking for someone to apologize for hiding Reg's stuff, but no one owned up, obviously.

'I'd like to say that I think it's unfair a *certain* bastard,' Nick said, glancing at me, 'is accusing me of doing something when I'm totally innocent. It's *humiliating*.'

71

'OK, Nick,' I said. 'If you didn't do it, then I apologize.' That was the best I could manage, given I was sure he was guilty, almost certainly alongside Peter.

'Let's move on,' said Toby. 'I think you know the general pattern of these expeditions. We have four training days first, and then we start our challenge. You're all on the Ultimate Bushcraft Gold Star Challenge, which means we'll be trekking through remote territory inland from here. This isn't about five-star hotels, you'll be really experiencing the great Aussie outdoors, making your own fires, cooking your own food, sometimes camping outside. It's a once-in-a-lifetime chance to do something closer to nature – living on the edge.'

'It all sounds a bit scary to me,' said Luke, evidently both excited and worried.

'I'm sure there's a structured plan,' said Lee.

'Yeah, it's all organized. There's no mobile reception where we're going, no Wi-Fi or public toilets, but we have to be at a set point each night and the cabins all have a radio or a telephone.'

'What if there's an emergency?' asked Luke.

'Like a broken fingernail?' muttered Peter.

'We're never more than ten miles from a contact point, and never too far from farms and roads. It's a radical trip, but it's all been checked out and risk-assessed. Keeping you safe is our number one priority.'

I looked over at Reg, who had been silent since getting his clothes back, and promised myself that I'd look out for him. He was one of the good guys.

'And finally,' said Toby, 'about tomorrow: we do some of our challenge in canoes down a river, so we'll be training in the sea. I presume everyone's happy with that?'

There were a lot of enthusiastic noises, but Lee looked serious and put his hand up.

'Yeah, Lee, shoot,' said Toby.

There was silence for about three or four seconds while Lee breathed in and out through his nose deeply. Then: 'I'm afraid I can't swim very well. I defy the laws of physics,' he said.

'What, mate? You can't swim?' Jason said. '*Everyone* can swim. You said that you could on the permission form.'

Lee was red-faced. It was the first time I'd seen him unsure of exactly what to say, but he quickly gathered his wits. 'I suppose I can swim underwater, given that that's where I normally end up. OK, I formally confirm that I can swim like a fish.'

I thought that was a clever way out of it, but my chuckle got lost in the laughter and insults.

'I think you'll be all right,' said Toby. 'We'll all be wearing life jackets, and we'll start with some training about how to move around in the water when you have one on. Jase and I will be there in single-man canoes. Don't worry, mate, we'll keep an eye on you.' He stood up. 'Now, we're all shattered after the journey, so grab some food and then head off to bed.'

While we grabbed food off the barbecue, Peter asked about the girls who were in another, similar, house nearby.

'Yeah, the girls have to join us for some of the training and there's a barbecue with them tomorrow night,' said Jason.

There were whoops and comments about this, all positive, mostly rude. Reg, happier by the minute, even said, 'Bring it on!'

'Yeah! Let me at 'em,' said Nick. 'I've got a lot to offer a girl.'

'Where's their house?' asked Peter.

'It's through the trees, before the next inlet,' said Toby. Perhaps there was a little amusement in his voice, but I couldn't be sure. 'But it's time for some sleep now. Shake off that jet lag. No one's to leave the house. You'll need all your energy tomorrow for the canoeing.'

'And for the barbecue the girls will be having with me.' Nick smirked.

Soon after, we drifted inside. I remember turning just before the door and looking out to sea, listening to the sound of waves gently lapping in the total black of the night. Two people were visible on the very edge of the light that was thrown out by the house.

Just for an instant I saw one person holding the shoulders of another and whispering in his ear. One of them tall and thin, the other shorter and unable to stand still. I didn't stop to think about it; I was so tired and it didn't register as important at the time.

[Here ends the sixth part of George's statement]

THE OTHER CHAPTER 6
(SAID IN THE HOUR BEFORE):
HIM

I remember how you were given a room on your own. Typical. Bias. I can't stand <u>favouritism</u>. I've been around the world, me, and I've seen that everyone is EQUAL. Until they make themselves unequal.

And some of us are *more* than equal.

The snivelling apologies to you on the bus. *Oh, Georgey, I love you and I'm sorry. Oh, Georgey, I love you and want to have your babies.* <u>Favouritism</u>.

Typical of *Georgey* to have such a <u>pathetic</u> puppet. You were always trying to humiliate people.

I couldn't resist taking the clothes. It served Reggie right for taking up so much space. No one admired Reg's body. Not even Reg. But I'm *sure* I saw you admiring *my* body – I'm right, aren't I?

HEY – YOU. Don't drift away from me. WAKE UP.

. . .

Look at me now.

WAKE UP.

WAKE UP.

IT MAKES ME SO BLOODY ANGRY WHEN YOU DON'T
DO WHAT I SAY.

Please. Don't. Make. Me. Do. Something. **You'll**. Regret.
Now.

Beautiful scar, isn't it? It's shaped like a rainbow. Isn't
it?

You know how I got that?

That was my dad. The thing that absolutely makes me <u>kill</u>
myself laughing is that *this* was a complete accident. All the
times that bastard hit me and hurt me and he didn't leave a
mark, and then this was a slip on the floor and a smash of
the glass and . . .

THAT HAPPENED. Scarred for life.

Blood spurted across the room.

Someone at school told me there's a line in a poem by
some old geezer about how parents screw you up. I bet your
parents were all soft, soft like the inside of an insect. My
parents were METAL. And MENTAL.

Anyway – you are ALWAYS distracting me, and we don't
have forever.

Taking the clothes was a job *very* well done, don't you
think? Just the right place to leave them as well. Rubbish
with the rubbish. A work of <u>genius</u>.

And that's what I am – an **<u>absolute</u>** *genius*!

Think of everything I've achieved: only a GENIUS could have done all this.

I suppose you think that I did it all on my own. You still don't know who my accomplice was? It was the start of a very useful partnership. You're so thick in the head. STUPID.

And by the end of the day I had <u>another</u> very useful puppet, with fear as my strings. Someone who could not resist. Someone to serve me, just as *Georgey* had servants to assist him.

You make me angry, Georgey. And when I get angry I <u>need</u> to hurt someone.

But I want to preserve you for a little while longer.

STATEMENT #6

ANDREA BROWN

I can confirm that the room arrangements at the Thorpe Cove boys' house were as follows:

George Fleet was sharing with **Matthew** Lough (after the latter's arrival)

Lee Andrews was sharing with **Luke** Bertrand

Alastair Boyd was sharing with **Reginald** Sanworth

Nicholas McGregor was sharing with **Peter** Emsworth-Lyle

Toby Jones and **Jason** Bayne had separate rooms at either end of the building.

I have been asked to restate for the record that Toby Jones was sometimes out of the main building and with me in the girls' house, about half a mile away, and that I visited the boys' house a few times, sometimes with the girls' group and sometimes on my own. But this didn't happen all the time. Toby was *always* very serious about his duties.

I sent some texts home but was so soundly asleep two minutes later that I didn't hear the pings of the replies. The next morning I was still fast asleep when Luke was sent in to wake me up.

'You must have been having bad dreams,' he said, shaking the side of the bunk. 'You twitch a lot in your sleep.'

'Morning,' I mumbled, cloudy with sleep. 'Is it time to get up? I don't remember any bad dreams – something about swimming, maybe?'

'It looked like a nasty dream to me. Probably something to do with spiders or snakes.' Luke stared into my eyes. 'Jason told me to tell you that it's time for breakfast.'

Toby was talking as I arrived outside at the logs. '. . . no further than the headland, and the tide would bring you in. Hey, George, mate, you'll be happy with this news: Matt's joining us this arvo.'

I smiled. 'Good.'

'Fancy some breakfast?' said Reg. He handed me

scrambled eggs with doorstep-sized toast, and said, quietly: 'Thanks for trying to help yesterday. I got stressed cos I was annoyed. But you and Alastair have been really nice about everything.' Then, not much more than a whisper, 'I can't help being fat, you know – it's a medical thing.'

'I did say I wanted us to be mates,' I said, and we shook hands.

Peter interrupted at this point. 'He'll let you give him a kiss if you ask nicely.'

Then it was Nick. 'Probably let you do more than that.'

Peter, straight after, laughing: 'Especially if he loses his clothes again.'

'Now come on, guys,' said Toby, trying, I thought, to cajole Peter and Nick into being pleasant. 'We've got a massive day in front of us. I'll do a bit of land training with the canoes first, then we'll head out into the bay and get some practice. It's harder here than down the river, where the current takes you and you just have to steer away from the rocks at the side. Now, get inside, slap on the suncream, and come out in trunks in half an hour. Helmets and life jackets are in the crate.'

As everyone wandered inside, the sun already throwing down heat, Toby called me back. 'Hey, George,' he said. 'There's an odd number and I wondered if you'd mind taking a single canoe out. They're a bit more inclined to flip, but I gather you're a –' he paused to make the most of the backward compliment – 'a *half-decent* swimmer.' He was smiling when he said it, being really nice as usual.

I said that wasn't a problem and smiled back. Jason watched us, not looking very happy, even tutting a little, but I wasn't sure why. Toby had come to me, and not the other way round, after all.

We really did start with the basics: putting on the life jacket and what to do in an emergency. Of course, when the emergency did happen that afternoon, none of the procedures were followed, but that wasn't Toby's fault and he did what he had to do to the letter.

Then we sat in the canoes on land. I got some hassle about being in a canoe on my own ('George is in a canoe with all his friends'), but it was only from Nick and Peter so it was easy to shrug off.

Reg put up with some banter about whether the canoe would float with him in it, but Lee went on about the boat dropping lower in the water and being more stable, which I *think* was meant to be kind.

'Low in the water is about right – probably about thirty feet underwater,' was Nick's quip. He was really beginning to annoy me, but that was nothing compared to what happened in the afternoon.

(I want to tell this in some detail.)

Matt hadn't returned by lunchtime (I was hoping that he would suddenly arrive so that we could share a boat), and Jason split up the canoes so that they weren't based on dorms. That seemed sensible as it broke up Nick and Peter. Reg went with Luke, and Nick with Al (I felt that Alastair didn't want that, but that was just a belief at the time because I had taken against Nick). Reg and Luke were messing about, pretending to be Olympic athletes limbering up.

The really important bit was that Peter, who declared himself a good swimmer (*bring it on!* I thought) went with Lee, who was still really sensitive about not being able to swim much, if at all.

We all clambered into the boats and played around near the shore. Steering was difficult at first, but I soon got the hang of the single boat and the others figured out how to work together rather than hindering one another. Toby and Jason weaved between the boats, shouting instructions and encouragement, as well as doing a fair bit of mocking, comparing our efforts to what their mothers and grandmothers could achieve.

There were races between the two-man boats, but

as Nick and Alastair won by ever-increasing margins, enthusiasm for competition evaporated.

It was after this, when Toby said that we could have some free time with the boats, that things began to go wrong. All of us, including Toby and Jason, drifted further from the shore and therefore out of the bay – it was just a few hundred yards but that made all the difference to the size of the waves. Reg started using his paddle to splash Nick's boat, but Nick and Alastair were quick and retaliated by swooping in, splashing, and then paddling away really quickly. Even Lee became more and more confident on the water. It was good fun while it lasted.

All the time, we floated further round the headland and towards the rocks outside the bay.

We probably would have avoided problems had someone not spotted the girls on the rocks. There were eight of them with two leaders – I could just about make out Andrea as one of the adults. This added showing off into the mix. I'll admit to joining in and paddling a bit harder. Who wouldn't? Some of the girls were in bikinis. I think we all wanted to be noticed ahead of the barbecue.

Toby then tried to call everyone back, but Reg and Luke weren't listening, and the other two boats had the alpha-male edge of Nick and Peter.

'Get back, now!' he shouted. But no one listened.

Nick and Alastair then rammed Peter and Lee's boat. Nick was obviously the one egging Alastair on. 'Ram! Ram! Ram!' he shouted. It wasn't exactly the collision that capsized the other boat – that was caused by Peter and Lee reaching out to retaliate, but it would never have happened without Nick's stupidity. With a shout and a muddle of arms and legs that looked like a fight in a cartoon, Peter and Lee capsized.

Lee flailed his arms around in wild panic, sending himself further out to sea. He was shouting so loudly and was in such a state that it was impossible to get any message through, though both Toby and Jason tried to as they raced off to try to rescue him.

The bizarre and unexpected thing was that Peter, who no one was very worried about, didn't resurface for ages, and then when he did it was without his lifebelt and in a completely different place. He was splashing around and gurgling, in a total panic, nowhere near his boat.

Stupidly, I just sat there for about five seconds before I realized Peter couldn't swim either. The idiot had told us a pack of lies about how good he was. There was no hope of him returning to his boat and using it for buoyancy, which was the logic Toby had drilled into us.

I paddled over really quickly, but there was nothing I could do from the boat. Every time I got near, Peter's whirling arms pushed my canoe away.

I still don't know what the most sensible thing to do would have been, but it probably wasn't taking off my lifebelt, which is exactly what I did (my mind was racing – I thought the lifebelt was an obstacle that would get in the way of swimming properly). I capsized the canoe, which was harder than it sounds, and slid out underwater. It actually only took me five or six swimming strokes to get to Peter, who was still thrashing around.

As I reached out to try to help him, one of his arms smacked me round the ear, and then another punched me in the lip (I realized that this was unintentional).

I had to swim behind him and, as he weakened, I somehow managed to hold both his arms to his side while keeping us afloat by kicking my legs.

'Just stop moving and I can help you! Stop moving! Come on – I'm trying to help you!' I swore at him really badly which was unusual for me – I suppose I was worried he would whack me round the head and knock me out.

Eventually he stopped moving and I could use one arm to start moving us and use Peter's buoyancy as a strength, but it was still the most difficult thing I've ever done in water. Peter was tall but thin, more bone than muscle, despite his boasting. I kept on dipping underwater and rising up into a confused salty spray. I could hear the roaring of the waves and shouting – possibly at me, maybe at Peter. Sky and sea and land all came in random order as I concentrated on kicking with my legs and stretching out with my free arm, just as I had practised in the pool back at home. But it was so much more difficult in the sea, straining against the current, worrying that Peter would slip away and sink like a stone.

Peter was silent now. I still shouted at him when I could, waves and breathlessness permitting, wanting to know that he was still conscious.

Then we entered the relative calm of the bay and I yanked Peter towards the bay kick by kick. Every thrust brought a deeper ache of tight muscle; every pull of my arm strained my shoulder. I dipped under the water and tasted salt. It wasn't fun.

We more or less floated the last few yards towards the shore, carried by the waves like two corks. It was Peter who stood up first – my own legs crumpled when my feet touched the sand and I let myself sink under the water for a few seconds.

The girls had moved from the rocks along the path into

our bay and some were paddling out through the water towards us. Andrea and the other helper in the girls' group were closest, coming to help us to the shore, and it was Andrea who helped me up.

When I rose, there was shrieking, whooping and cheering from the girls, like an orchestra gone wrong. My face reddened, and not just because of the exertion.

As I strode through the water trying to make it look as if this was the sort of thing I did all the time, one of the girls – I didn't know her name then, of course, but it was Zara – put her hands behind her head and fell into the shallow water, saying, 'Save me!' as she fell. As good as this was in one way, after the previous rescue on the plane, and the stuff with Reg, I knew that the hero worship wouldn't go down well with the other guys.

Behind me, Toby was steaming in, arms straining powerfully, his canoe slightly raised up at the front, with a now calm Lee clinging on to a short rope that ran from the back of the boat. I had somehow beaten them to the shore. The remaining canoes circled around like sharks. You would think that the other guys would have been pleased and relieved, maybe shocked, but it wasn't entirely like that. True, Reg applauded and Luke cheered like a little kid – over the top, though probably not to mock – but Nick's face was like thunder and Alastair's was expressionless.

Peter was muttering to himself, grandly shrugging away any help, saying that it was all a fuss over nothing and implying, and then actually *saying* that he would have been fine if only I had left him alone. He never said thanks – not in any way, not *ever*. He was so aloof. He wouldn't even look at me properly.

But returning with incredible timing was Matt. He was standing on the shore with a big grin on his face, hands above his head, clapping. A taxi driver was standing next to his luggage.

The scene has stuck in my head, even down to the smallest detail, but I can't properly recall the next ten or fifteen minutes, probably because of the attention from the girls and my exhaustion. The next thing I remember was sitting on the logs with bikini-clad girls either side of me, with Matt retelling the story of what had happened on the plane. I *pretended* to be modest – but I have to admit it, I loved the attention, every bit of it.

'It's so impressive!' said Zara. 'Saving one person is, like, really good, but saving three is, like, triply amazing.'

Her friend, Belle, short for Annabel, sat with her arm

draped over my shoulder. 'Tense your muscles,' she said, and giggled when I did.

The afternoon drifted into evening and the barbecue was lit. I lapped up the girls' attention, far more interested in them than the other boys, apart from Matt. And, to be honest, I didn't feel he was a rival, so I was comfortable sharing the limelight.

To have girls like Zara and Belle interested in you is like a drug. They were pretty and intelligent – any boy would have enjoyed it. If you think I was overwhelmed by having these girls making a fuss over me, you're right. (I realize now that I should have handled it all better, and brought people like Reg into the conversation.)

The other boys – apart from Matt, who had managed to be next to Belle – were on the outskirts of the action. I think they spoke to some of the other girls, but perhaps that seemed small consolation for someone like Nick, who couldn't drag his eyes away from Belle, though I'm not sure anyone else noticed.

I remember that Toby was talking to Andrea all the time, while Jason chatted uneasily with Andrea's helper, and sometimes with Peter and Luke and the others.

Peter kept well away from me. As I said, he didn't even once say thanks. Not even grudgingly.

Luke chirped away with one or two girls who clearly liked him. But sometimes he gazed into space, dreaming or scheming, I didn't know.

Lee didn't seem to know how to talk to girls casually, but was telling one about the currents in the bay. He didn't speak to me.

And Alastair muttered to Reg in between making nearby girls laugh. But he also didn't speak to me. And Reg, he seemed so uncomplicated – innocent Reg.

I had no idea that one of them was plotting something terrible.

[Here ends the seventh part of George's statement]

THE OTHER CHAPTER 7
(SAID IN THE HOUR BEFORE):
HIM

I WAS going to talk about how annoying you were that first night, to get it all in the open, and discuss it man to man, and let my feelings flood out, but seeing your pathetic eyes now – such sad, stupid eyes – I think that JUSTICE has been served.

[Pause]

WHAT WAS THAT? Did I hear you say something? GO ON – I dare you to say it again.

GO ON – say that right into my ear.

I'm listening.

WELL?

. . .

NO. I am _not_ a murderer. I am no more a murderer than a fisherman or a farmer.

I WAS FORCED TO DO THIS BY GEORGEY'S BEHAVIOUR.

GEORGEY'S behaviour.

It was after the first day of training that I knew I was going to HAVE to do something for the good of everyone.

First you saved someone from the warm tongue of a

fire – so predictable. Then you forced yourself into the action on the plane – sickening.

And

THEN

to interfere when someone couldn't swim – there's no harm in not being able to swim; we don't all <u>have</u> to be great swimmers, do we?

DO WE? That was just dick-waving in front of the girls. Georgey the dick. Waver.

And I could see that Georgey's DISEASE was infectious. That BLOODY SICKENING show afterwards – it was like a witch doctor hypnotizing his victims.

The worst bit? When you got out of the water and slithered up the beach with your hands all over those girls. They weren't interested in you **really**, **Georgey**, they were just hypnotized – hyp-no-tized – ooooooh . . .

The idea of a man touching a woman in that way. It's disgusting.

ZARA. She was corrupted by Georgey's sickness. And Annabel. Especially Annabel.

Men should leave women alone.

I want you to bloody well <u>agree</u> that I had no choice. I had to cut out the disease. And first you have to start by clearing out the infection. I was nothing more than a *good doctor*.

The other boys were being corrupted as well, though they pretended to give you the hate you deserved. I sensed them slowly being sucked in. And I know you sensed it too, though you pretended not to. They were sucked in. Sluuuurp.

I had to be the good surgeon. I couldn't let the virus spread. No way, José.

Yeah, that was when I started to plan. It was when I listened to that bell-end, smarmy Toby, that I knew I'd have to take every opportunity to do a good job. I've done well, haven't I?

And now the job is nearly done. Just YOU to finish with.

Thank you. You bow before me. *All hail the king.*

BUT

don't – don't – never – get me started on Toby. He was the first of Georgey's followers, the first of his slaves. He probably *fancied* you.

So I had a slave and you had a slave.

Actually, I had slave<u>s</u>. You never realized that, did you? But you should bear it in mind while you hear my story.

I HOPE YOU ARE PAYING ATTENTION.

Me and my followers.

Yep. I would cut out the disease. And a doctor prescribes **medicine**. HA! HA! You never knew about my medicine!

It all went so well until you tried to take over, like a slug that springs back into shape after you remove your foot. *(But a slug I admire a little bit.)*

Then it was a duel of wits. Could Georgey work it out?

And now look at me. I am the winner. I AM THE CENTRE OF THE UNIVERSE.

I HAVE THE POWER OF LIFE AND DEATH OVER <u>YOU</u>.

EVIDENCE #1

EXTRACTED FROM AN EMAIL
SENT BY ZARA NEVES

Hiya girls how much is it raining? Hot hot hot here. Having fun with the mad team. It's just how you imagine it with sand and sea and sun.

No sex (yet!!!!!!!) but have met this great guy. He's a real-life hero (saved another guy's life in front of our eyes!!!) and really nice and funny. Probs a bit too nice to get anywhere with. Has a girlfriend, I think (but doesn't sound serious............). Faint at the pic!!!!!!!!!!!!! Fit!!!!!!!!!!!!!!!!!! Get this – he lives in Southend, near my cousins.

. . .

Will be in the outback soon, so you'll have to wait for the next episode of this real-life Neighbours. Keep thinking of me down under.

Lots of love

Zara xxxxxxxxxx ☺

CHAPTER 8
(FIVE DAYS BEFORE):
THE EIGHTH PART OF
GEORGE'S STATEMENT

I need to tell the second day of training as it was, but now I understand so much more.

The day was spent at Climbers' Kingdom. Despite the silly name – weird because there were also things like archery in a sports hall – it was a pretty cool place.

All the awkwardness of the previous evening was lost over breakfast, where everyone (apart from Luke, who always seemed to be full of energy) was levelled by tiredness, and on the minibus, where Jason led us in some chants. This showed a new side to Jason. I had seen him as a slightly annoying sidekick to Toby, but he really got into teaching us the choruses and singing the verses himself.

Toby looked uncomfortable – probably because some of the lyrics were sexist and others rude about people. I didn't want the guys to think that I was some sort of monk as well as Toby's pet, so I joined in with some of it. Anyway, some of it was properly funny.

*

97

'We're really lucky, guys,' said Toby when we arrived. 'We've got all the best activities.'

He was right. The most 'high-octane', as they called it, was probably the first one – a sort of bungee jump that lets you fall down and forward into the air like a swing – called the 4G Swing (it was meant to be the same as experiencing four Gs – 'As you fall, it feels like four times the usual gravity of the Earth, of course,' as Lee explained). You then swung back and forth like a pendulum, gradually losing momentum. Two went on at a time. Matt and I both volunteered to go with Reg, who was hassled by Nick and Peter about how he was likely to break the bungee rope. Stupid, since adults had been on it.

In the end, to my amazement, Nick ended up pairing with Reg on the first go, though he made a meal of it, wailing about how afraid he was.

'A magnificent experiment,' said Lee, hands behind his back and hair sticking out like a mad scientist. 'This is better than CERN: larger particles to smash together.'

I went with Lee. We were harnessed and attached to a thick metal strip, then winched up by the other boys pulling on a rope. There were three levels: green, amber and red. But no one opted for anything other than red. The harness tugged in the worst possible place as you were heaved upwards. Most of the cries at this stage were about bruised balls and squeezed sacs and crushed . . . you get the idea.

But Lee was different. As we went higher off the ground, the science-based humour changed to something creepier. 'Imagine what it would be like to hit the ground,' he whispered. 'You would know it was going to happen, but be unable to stop it.'

'Shut it, man,' I said. 'You're freaking me out.'

'And then there would be one instant when you tried to go through the ground but couldn't.'

'Help, I want to get off!' I said, half joking.

There was mockery from below. 'You're not in the water now,' someone shouted. 'Pull them as high as possible,' said someone else.

'You're not in the water now,' Lee repeated. 'Oh no – you can't get off.' Then, lips brushing my ear, a chill in his voice: 'If this goes wrong, enjoy the nanosecond between your feet and your head hitting the ground.'

'Lee, don't be so—'

But the rest of what I said became a scream. It was brilliant: weightless falling, stomachs left behind; then the bungee line strained as we were guided away from the ground and forward into thin air, to just over 45 degrees, like a playground swing that had gained a lot of speed. As with all the previous riders, we swore loudly.

Then we were pulled backwards, relaxing slightly, shouts coming from below, and then forward and back, calmer and calmer, until after about six or seven swings we stopped near the ground.

A metal trolley was then wheeled out for us to stand on and get off. Luke pushed it forward.

'Here comes the trolley dolly,' Nick said.

'That was awesome,' whooped Lee. 'The fear is *so* exciting. Epic. There's nothing like it.'

Looking back, I wish I had told someone about his weirdness as we were winched up, but, caught in the moment, I smiled and laughed.

The only person who didn't make any excited sounds as he went up or down was Luke. While waiting, he seemed nervous, waving his hands even when he *wasn't* speaking. But Luke was made of ice when hoisted up. 'Send us as high as possible,' he said on his second turn, with Reg. 'Right to the very top.'

I looked carefully as he fell. His eyebrows were slightly raised and he was half smiling. Completely calm. A different person.

The moment he stepped off, he was energized again,

springing around as he said, 'It was orgasmatronic!'

Luke was exactly the same on the other highlight of the morning: The Vertical Assault Course. We did this after Abseiling and Leap of Faith (a jump to a triangle from the top of a pole).

The Vertical Assault Course was a collection of logs, ladders and walls either built up from the ground or suspended from above by wires. You progressed along it from left to right. Some of it was only just off the ground, but other parts were seriously high. It was all 'perfectly safe' because a metal wire ran along the very top, our harnesses attached to it by a safety rope.

It was impossible to do it on your own. One of you had to be the leader and the other the follower, so that the safety wires didn't get tangled as you moved along.

Nick and Matt were the pair before me. Matt was fairly useless, not very well coordinated and of no help to Nick. Not that Nick needed his help. He raced through the course, even the more difficult bits, including the parts that were meant to be impossible to do on your own. At the top of the final section, he stood tall and showed off his muscles. Matt was barely halfway there.

My partner was Luke. He was slightly smaller than everyone else (Nick had taken to calling him 'Stick Man') but his bony appearance was slightly misleading: it was obvious from his showing on Leap of Faith that he could climb like a monkey.

The harness was put on by an instructor called Jake, a tall, tough-looking man with an earring and nose stud. He was helped by a girl whose name I can't remember and am still trying to find out. It was then checked by Toby and/or Jason – and I'm pretty sure both examined mine, but I was busy looking at the Vertical Assault Course and talking strategy with Luke. We agreed that Luke would be the leader and I would follow.

Before starting on the 45-degree rising log that led to the rest of the assault course, we all gave the participants high fives and bear hugs that were almost a wrestle. 'You can do it, yeah!' was the sort of thing that was said.

'Good luck, man,' said Peter, who was standing next to Jason. Then, I'm sure, in a mumble: 'You're gonna need it.' I remember it because there was a slightly-too-long pause in the middle: *Good luck, man* – silence, looking into my eyes – then: *you're gonna need it*, as I turned away.

Just as before, Luke was gesticulating energetically, but he stopped the instant he was on the activity. He was definitely the better climber. I remember thinking he could be a free climber, scaling a cliff in a national park. I felt pretty cumbersome and timid by comparison.

With some other pairs, the safety ropes were a vital part of the ascent, used to help haul them skyward. But we were too good for that and went up like true climbers, the safety ropes slightly slack.

After the diagonally rising log – which was easily wide enough to walk up – there was a section that was like rock climbing. I didn't look down. Luke raced ahead.

Next there was a horizontal beam to walk along. This would have been fine a few inches off the ground, but being thirty feet in the air does things to your mind.

All those things were OK.

We then went down a ladder before going up something called Stairway to Heaven. This was seven horizontal logs, suspended by wire at both ends, arranged one on top of the other, about three or four feet apart at first. We clambered and tugged and heaved and pushed, Luke and me, helping one another, again without needing our safety ropes to drag us up.

Soon we only had the very top log to reach. As all the logs were held together by wire through the ends, they moved about like hell. The top log was about five feet from the log below, so I knelt as still as I could, one knee raised for Luke to stand on, then he scrambled off my shoulder on to the log above. That meant he had reached the very top, forty feet off the ground – high enough for the staring faces below to look no bigger than coins. One person was holding up a phone, recording every detail. If his smashed phone is ever repaired you will see this is true.

Without anyone to step on, it was more difficult for me. The plan was for me to swing one leg over and have Luke pull me up. More than once my leg slipped and we had to start again. Eventually, I wrapped both legs round the thick log and Luke manhandled me on to the upper side of the log. He was stronger than he looked.

Then (I feel giddy as I remember):

I stood up on the top log, alongside Luke. Suddenly there was a tug on one of the belt loops of my trousers and the metal hook at the end of the safety rope whacked against my chin. I remember looking down and seeing that a loop on my belt had been ripped. I took a sharp intake of breath and my insides shrank. I couldn't make sense of it. The safety rope had been attached to a belt loop on my trousers and not to my harness. It didn't compute. Unbelievable! At the time I said much worse, and loudly.

Because the rope hadn't been tugged properly earlier I'd no idea when it had become unattached, or even if it was properly attached in the first place, though I thought I had a vague memory of holding my arms out while it was pulled on my harness as a check.

The safety rope slithered madly upwards. I tried to grasp at it, but it was gone too quickly, wiggling like a crazy thing as it disappeared up to the top wire and then fell down the other side.

I was now completely unsupported on a log forty feet in the air.

Terrified, I did what was natural: straight away, I dropped down and wrapped myself round the log, becoming completely rigid, arms and legs like rock. The smallest movement was petrifying. You might think that I was still swearing, but I wasn't. I gave myself whispered guidance: 'Just stay perfectly still and you'll be fine; this is just a matter of time; don't crack under pressure.'

Luke, still suspended by his safety rope, sat legs either side of the log, and said, 'You haven't fallen. They'll come to get you.' Then quietly: 'I'm sorry.' At least, I thought that's what he said, but the boys below were shouting and I was concentrating so hard on staying calm that I couldn't be sure.

Being on the upper side of the log, I was looking down, of course, and that made things a lot worse. Closing my eyes made it more difficult to keep my balance. Gradually

I relaxed and realized that I wouldn't fall if I actually kept my cool, but a slight giddiness was creeping in from the corners of my brain, and I couldn't keep it back.

I concentrated on keeping my breathing shallow. It was the same drill as when you're swimming: in through your nose, out through your mouth; keep calm and stay the course.

I then found myself slipping round the log: it was like I couldn't get my bearings and was confused about how to balance myself. The log was smooth and not very thick (probably about four adult hands could have spanned it) and in trying to correct the movement I overcompensated and slipped round underneath.

Imagine what it would be like to hit the ground, I recalled Lee saying. *You would know it was going to happen, but be unable to stop it.*

'Hold on, Georgey,' said Luke. 'They're on their way.'

I didn't need anyone to tell me to hold on. Upside down, I clung on to that log with every fibre in my body, folding my arms and interlocking my feet so that they couldn't slip free. Slowly, I angled my head round and saw Jake, the instructor, leaping powerfully up the logs, a safety rope in one hand. He was shouting as he climbed: 'Stay calm, George. Don't move.'

'I'm not planning on moving!' I hollered back. 'But it'd be good if you hurried.' This bravado was pretty much an act, but deep down I knew that if I didn't panic things would probably turn out OK. I saw myself from the outside, as if I was two people – one of them sensible and logical and advising the other.

When Jake arrived, he stood on the top log and threw the safety rope over the wire that ran above everything and then collected the end with the metal hook when it dangled down the far side.

'Any time now would be good,' I said, sensing that rescue was near and determined to come out of it with a good reputation. To think like that, I suppose, meant that I was back in control.

'You'll have to release yourself slightly from the log,' said Jake as he descended to the log below, 'so that I can attach this to your harness.'

As I tried to move my feet along the log towards my head, so that my waist would dip and create a space for Jake to attach the metal clasp of the safety rope to my harness, one foot slipped. Then the other slipped too. I know it sounds like a cliché, but it did seem to happen frame by frame, slow enough for me to be aware of what was happening, cling on even tighter with my arms, and aim my feet on to the log below. Incredibly, they plonked straight on to the log, and Jake clipped on the rope a second later. I was safe, and soon being winched down, heart pumping, holding tightly to the rope even though I knew – this time – that it was securely attached to my harness.

Everyone applauded, including Luke, who was also descending. It's chilling to know *now* that everyone included some seriously nasty people. At the time, it just seemed like a freak near-accident.

At the bottom there were men in ties (looking worried) as well as a couple of first-aiders rushing in. 'Are you all right?' one asked.

'Better than I would have been if I'd fallen,' I said.

Jake, the instructor, was white-faced and shaking slightly. I told him that it was an accident and my fault. I thought I had somehow made a mistake, but knew he might have been careless. I never considered the possibility that someone had tried to kill me. I never imagined that keeping calm here was training for what happened later. And I never told my parents about what happened: I knew they would have worried. I did mention it to Jess, though.

After about fifteen minutes my heart rate returned to normal, but I still had to endure an irritating hour of form filling and medical checks. Finally I pleaded with them to let me go – I wasn't harmed and didn't want to waste the opportunity to get on and do other things. I also remembered a bit of advice my dad gave me when I was doing some tricks on my bike when I was about eleven: *if you fall off, try to get back on as soon as possible, otherwise you'll lose your bottle.* I knew we had Zip Wire at 2.30 p.m. and was determined to give it a go.

Zip Wire certainly did the trick to get my confidence back. I heard a lot of encouragement – on reflection, some of it a bit forced, perhaps – and I did it the same as I always would have, apart from three or four extra checks that the metal clasp at the end of the safety rope was firmly attached to my harness this time.

'Yeah! Yeah! Yeah!' I shouted as I descended, wind gusting against my face, lost in the moment, absolutely loving it.

The final activity of the day was archery. I was talking to one of the instructors, so was late leaving Zip Wire. As I walked to the archery I saw a jersey that looked like Reg's hanging over the wooden fence, so I ran to pick it up. It was ridiculous that he had brought it on a baking-hot day, but I didn't want him to think he'd lost any more clothes. By fluke, this meant I looked down the back of the sports hall, a large corrugated-metal building, and saw Peter and Luke. Peter had Luke by the hair and was pushing him against the side of the sports hall and speaking really aggressively to him, about two inches from his face.

Peter stopped almost as soon as he saw me. He gave Luke one more shove, then walked away, barging my shoulder as he passed. I was determined to stand my ground. 'I can't stand boys like him,' he said, pointing in the vague direction of Luke, as he strode off into the distance.

Luke's shoulders drooped as he approached me. There were tears and confusion in his eyes.

'You OK, Luke?' I asked.

He sagged further. 'I'm OK. I hope you're gonna to be OK.'

'What do you mean?'

'It's . . . Never mind. Just remember that I told you to be careful.' Luke kept on walking.

'What's that s'posed to mean?' I said. 'Come on. Tell me.'

'Just remember . . .' I didn't catch anything else as Luke broke into a jog that turned into a sprint. Seconds later he disappeared down the path towards the archery.

I went into the archery with low expectations, but it

was actually all right. Luke snapped out of his depression almost immediately and wouldn't stop talking. It was at this point that everyone started calling me 'Georgey'. I couldn't complain: nicknames for others had been made over the past few days – Luke was *Stick Man*, Reg was *Chubbs*, and so on – and it would have annoyed everyone if I'd moaned. But I'm going to continue using everyone's real name, even in speech.

A cry of 'Well done, Georgeeeeeey!' would go up every time I hit the target.

The only slightly unpleasant thing was Lee talking about death again – or, to be really precise, now I've had time to think about it – talking about *dying*. 'If they didn't hit any vital organs, I wonder how many arrows it would take to kill a man.' The others actually spent some time discussing this, gruesome though it was. Matt and I didn't take it seriously and he kept on cracking jokes: 'My dick could probably absorb twenty strikes,' and that sort of thing. Good old Matt.

Matt was totally mal-coordinated and could hardly put the arrow on the bow, let alone hit the target. He became known as *Malco*.

Nick won the archery, a few points ahead of me. No one else could compete with us. Matt hit the target *once*, but he didn't care; even Reg was better than him.

Later, back at base, we met up with the girls again for another barbecue. It did seem to be true about Australians and barbecues. Andrea brought the girls over (they always came to us, we never went over to their place), and we gradually spread out over the whole beach in small groups, eating (very) burnt sausages and crispy corn on the cob. It all went according to plan for Matt and me. We had spoken before about trying to spend time with Zara and Belle.

I want to be clear that Jess is the girl I really love; she's the one I think about. I know that sounds a bit romcom now, but I know how I feel more than ever [thanks, Jess, for standing by me!]. I emailed her every day that I could from Australia – proper emails, explaining what had happened (minus some of the things I now know are important, and one thing that I will write about later, but including lots of other stuff). Those emails were totally different to the short notes I sent back to my parents.

But Matt and I found it much easier to get on with these girls than the other boys. It wasn't just that they were pretty, they were also nice and friendly. You didn't always have to prove something.

We talked about where we came from and why we were

on the trip. They knew about me because of what had happened in the bay. Matt told the story again of how he was on a beach with his parents and wandered off along the rocks ('because they were there and I was bored and sand was getting into places it shouldn't') when he found a kid in a massive panic halfway down the cliff.

'The brilliant thing is that my *pathetic* climbing – I'm the Malco Man – was explained in the papers as being calming. I was s'posed to have gone up and down slowly, nearly going arse over tit for the amusement of the young *scally*. Really, I was as scared as a naked nun in a nightclub. So as a reward for being a silly git I was sent out here to do more of what I couldn't do in the first place.'

'It sounds like a sick thing to do,' said Belle.

''Tis true I only really did it to impress the gals,' Matt joked. He had both of them rapt, though he was an unlikely sex god with his pointy nose and wild hair.

Conversation drifted on to films, then to music, and we finally ended up trying to tell a joke that was worse than the one before. All of Matt's were rude: 'How do you make a door squeak? You pull its knob' was probably the cleanest. That joke has stuck in my mind because it was at that point that Nick arrived.

I reckon that Nick had been drinking a fair bit. 'So,

ladies, when are you going to leave these w- [word deleted] alone and . . .' He then suggested they do something they found offensive.

Zara was savvy and seemed to have dealt with this sort of thing before. She suggested that Nick did the thing to himself, if he could find his dick.

Nick then lunged forward. 'How about a quick kiss, then?'

'Come on, let's go,' Matt said to Zara and Belle.

'You stay where you are, toss-pot,' slurred Nick.

Zara then told Nick to leave in the strongest language possible.

I thought that this was bound to end in a fight, probably with me.

Fortunately, Toby came jogging over, straight away put his arm firmly round Nick's shoulder, and guided him away.

'Get off me right now,' Nick said. 'I'm not *Georgey*. I don't want your hands all over me. You don't know what you're dealing with.'

I could see Jason and Peter in the distance, and it was to them that Nick returned after he had shrugged off Toby.

Immediately afterwards, Matt and I implied that we were about to sort Nick out. Zara and Belle claimed that *they* were about to sort him out (in fairness, Zara had looked fierce). And then I thought of a pathetic joke and we were cracking up again. It was the last good evening I had, and it went on late.

A lot of drinking had happened while we were at the far end of the beach (beer bottles were strewn everywhere) but everyone was inside apart from Reg, who was sat on his own listening to an iPod. I felt guilty that he had been left out.

The girls left. No kisses. Just a quick hug and 'see you tomorrow'.

I was tired, but Reg and I went to his room to try to get the Wi-Fi working.

I mention it because it meant that I saw Alastair's iPad – he had a brand-new one and insisted we used it rather than my clunky old machine. He had been drinking and didn't have much else to say that was sensible. It was when I typed something into Google that I saw his previous searches. Alastair was sitting opposite me and it felt like cheating or lying, but I couldn't stop myself viewing his search history. Some of it was weird stuff.

I remember that the words *torture* and *poison* leapt out.

[Here ends the eighth part of George's statement]

THE OTHER CHAPTER 8
(SAID IN THE HOUR BEFORE):
HIM

The way that you and that idiot Matt touched those girls was even more sickening on the second night. DISGUSTING. I had to drink myself senseless.

But the rest of the day was good. Goooooooooooooood.

'You're not in the water now!' I remember saying that as you stressed on the stupid swing. You were pathetic and helpless. But not as pathetic and helpless as you are right <u>NOW</u>.

While I was up there I enjoyed thinking about what it would be like to fall.

To

fall

down

THUMP!

Brains everywhere.

So I decided to make it as exciting as possible as soon as I had the chance. And my chance came on that stupid *Vertical Assault Course.*

I know you want to understand how it was all done.

<u>Luke</u> was made to do it.

And this is when you have to realize the genius you are dealing with. The level of my **immense** intelligence. The way in which I am <u>above</u> and <u>beyond</u> ordinary people. A *super*man. You don't know what you're dealing with.

Here you are, alone with me, thinking of ways to escape, and you have the dreadful and bone-chilling **realization** that <u>I</u> have been the PUPPET MASTER all along.

You see – I had found out why Luke was on the trip. It was a fluke that I knew – THANK YOU, GOD.

Mistreated by his parents. I know all about that. So I really knew the way to pull his strings and make him join in my little game.

And that made him an accomplice.

I mean, a slave.

Look at this on my camera.

[Camera plays]

Right <u>there</u>.

[Camera plays again]

See it. When he was pulling you up to the top log. It was eighteen seconds before you noticed.

[Camera plays for twenty seconds]

Now, that's <u>MAGIC</u>. YEAH!

Luke was *good*. He wasn't nearly as stupid as he seemed.

But then he started to have doubts – started to feel the stupidest thing in the world:

GUILT. Guilt. That pathetic hand that covers your mouth and stops you breathing. Stops you living.

He had to be controlled.

And <u>control</u> is my business. Isn't it?

<u>You</u> can hardly disagree. Given the position you're in.

Come on. Let me hear you say that you agree. Let me hear you say it, Georgey.

'YOU HAVE CONTROL OVER ME AND I'M HELPLESSLY UNDER YOUR TOTAL POWER.'

Not willing to say it?

Prefer to just sit there lazily?

I think you've made a mistake.

If they didn't hit any vital organs, I wonder how many arrows it would take to kill a man.

118

STATEMENT #7

JAKE AGLAROND

I was in charge of the Vertical Assault Course activity on the day that George Fleet and the others from Ultimate Bushcraft came. And, er, my job included safety.

I'm Level 4 trained – the highest level – I've never had a safety issue on anything before – never – other than on the day we're talking about.

We're trained to follow the exact same procedure – always checking the link to the harness by giving it a good tug. I remember doing that on the day you asked me to talk about.

George Fleet seemed a good bloke. I don't know how he managed to unclip his own link to the safety rope. But I'm told he was confused. Capable of doing stupid and horrible things while appearing normal. Not that I'm saying he's guilty. I'm just saying.

CHAPTER 9
(FOUR DAYS BEFORE):
THE NINTH PART OF
GEORGE'S STATEMENT

The third day of training was to do with survival in the wilderness.

It was the day that the first murder *started*. How easy that is to write: *It was the day that the first murder started.* The murder *started*. You'll see what I mean.

It also contained something personal that I feel bad writing about, but there's not much I can do as this is a factual account of events, written down for those who will judge me. I need to tell the truth.

The day was called Outback Survival. It was a series of activities that were supposedly preparing us for a week trekking through remote forests and hills. Preparing us? This wasn't even *nearly* true, but someone anticipating a gentle stroll in the countryside interrupted by fun tasks might have thought it was some sort of training. I'm sorry to sound bitter – that's not fair on Toby.

First we learnt how to make a fire. *Firecraft*. I felt uncomfortable, having been paired with Nick – but the strange thing was that Nick treated me as if we were best buddies, and we were good at fire-starting.

'Well done, boys,' said Jason as he passed.

'Yeah,' said Nick. 'We can burn down Australia. I'm the fire-making king.'

'I don't think so,' said Jason, pointing to steadily rising smoke a few hundred yards away. 'That's Al and Lee using just a thin reed and fireboard.'

As a pair, they were easily the best: Alastair was great at making Lee's ideas work.

The second activity was Communication: it was basically about attracting the attention of a passing aeroplane. Alastair and Lee again dominated, effectively taking over from Toby and Jason, explaining how light flashed from mirrors or a radio with nothing more than static could be used to send messages in Morse code.

'But what if you don't have a mirror or a radio?' said Luke.

'Then we'd use my torch,' said Alastair. 'It's more important to have a torch than a knife.'

'And we'd transmit in Morse like this . . .' Lee clapped his hands together in a strange pattern.

'That could mean anything,' said Luke, laughing, wide-eyed.

Lee clapped again, an even more complicated

rhythm, and longer this time.

'And what's that supposed to mean?' asked Luke, palms out, head on one side.

Lee looked pale with annoyance. 'It's what will happen to you if you question me again.'

I had no idea what Lee had Morsed, of course, or whether he was bluffing. I hated all this alpha-male stuff, which Lee was part of, in his own way.

Jason interrupted to say that everyone would have locator beacons in any case, but even they weren't really needed because of the satellite phones. 'But if anyone is stupid enough to wander off and finds a handy mirror, using it to reflect the sun into the eyes of a passing pilot would be a really clever idea.'

The third activity was all about Australian animals. The first part of this was spent telling us that there really wasn't much to worry about: that bees and horses killed more people in Australia than anything else. Toby said that almost no one dies from spider, shark, snake or croc bites – because people are careful and anti-venom has been developed for creatures like the funnel-web spider. But Oz still had some of the world's most venomous and aggressive animals. 'Like Jason,' he joked.

We spent a while talking about octopuses and jellyfish,

especially the box jellyfish, lethal, but fortunately out of season in July. Then it was snakes and spiders, the worst of which could kill within minutes. There were highly poisonous ones nearby: we just had to treat everything as if it was deadly, and stay well away. That's why we weren't shown many pictures – *everything* was dangerous.

And that was the problem with the talk in the light of what happened later. Being croc-safe was all about avoiding the creature, especially by staying out of certain parts of certain rivers; being snake-safe was all about making lots of noise and 'giving it a wide berth'. We weren't told what to do when you do come face to face with the things; we weren't told how to treat a victim of a bite from one. (I don't blame Toby – he was just doing what he had been told.)

The final activity before lunch was called Herbology. I didn't mention that I immediately recognized a Harry Potter reference, but Luke went crazy, jumping around and asking whether Pomona Sprout was going to teach us. There was general groaning about Harry Potter and comments about how it was boring. Luke didn't care, though, and started comparing everyone to Harry Potter characters: Reg was Hagrid; I remember that Matt was Ron. That was about right. 'Toby, you're . . . *Dumbledore*,' was met with general laughter because it was meant to be absurd, but I could see some weird similarities. Jason, with a finger pointed at him, was called 'Snape' (Jason did seem to have that combination of trying to be harsh and amusing at the same time).

Then he turned to Peter. There was a little pause for effect. 'And you're Draco Malfoy.'

Peter moved his head from side to side as if weighing it up, a smile on his face, but his eyes were unamused.

Luke turned to me. 'Georgey is a hero with everyone against him. He's got to be Harry Potter.'

The 'everyone against him' drained any satisfaction away from what was probably meant as a compliment.

There was a moment of silence and I felt embarrassed.

Then: 'He'd rather be Harry Styles,' said Matt, to laughter and my relief. Banter then restarted.

'OMG,' said Luke, trying to be as camp as possible. 'I simply *love* Wand Erection.'

That is how I remember Luke. An entertainer.

Herbology turned out to be interesting. It was about the plants that could be used for medicine or other practical purposes. If Toby was right, there was hardly anything that couldn't be healed by something somewhere in Australia.

The session dissolved into questions about illnesses

and what they could be cured with, and then into stupid questions about what other problems the herbs could deal with. Matt started it by asking about which herb could save you if you came into contact with a dingo. But that was funny because Matt had taken to calling a part of his body his 'dingo'. It was the way that Matt said it, with a comical wild-eyed stare.

'What can save you from a nuclear bomb?' asked Peter.

'What can save you from death by fatness?' said Nick.

'What can save you from a knife being plunged into here?' asked Alastair, pointing at his side. He was wearing a T-shirt, but I knew, and perhaps the others knew, too, that he was pointing at the very spot where his scar was. I wondered what had happened to him.

We were then warned by Toby and Jason about the plants that were dangerous: we had to be careful what we ate. We were told that there were a thousand plants in Australia that were toxic, and a hundred that could produce cyanide.

'Look out for this fella in particular: the strychnine tree – looks good enough to eat, but is also known as poison nut.' Toby showed us a picture, followed by another. 'And this is called angel's trumpets – but it's bloody *un*heavenly: this one will make you confused before killing you. And this little thing, oleander, will finish you off even if you put it on the fire and inhale the smoke. Eating it – fatal. And especially dangerous for kids. And they're the ones people in Sydney can find in their back garden.'

Toby then reeled off a number of other poisonous plants, and Jason held up pictures.

'Guys,' said Jason. 'The simple truth is that you shouldn't put anything in your mouth that you don't know everything about.'

Peter and Nick smirked. 'George and Matt, did you hear that?' said Peter, to excessive laughter from Nick.

Reg asked about our trip and what foods would be safe to eat.

Toby listed common things that sounded similar to what grows in England before explaining that all food would be provided. 'Foraging,' he said, 'is an important part of bushcraft, but this is a twenty-first-century trip. It'll be three meals a day.'

'Six meals in Reg's case,' said Nick. Peter laughed.

Reg seemed not to hear. 'Does any posh stuff grow out here, like caviar?' he asked.

Even I knew that caviar didn't grow on trees.

'Or spaghetti?' The words came out before I had a chance to stop them. 'Any spaghetti trees?' They were intended to shield Reg rather than make fun of him.

'What a thick shit,' said Peter, ignoring me and turning on Reg. 'You're too poor to eat caviar, in any case. But, if you do, it comes from a fish. A fish that looks a bit like you, but not as ugly.'

Nick's laughter was over the top, gurgling like a drain.

'Come on, Peter,' said Toby. 'That's out of order, man.'

'Yeah, come on, Pete,' Jason added. 'It's not right to *say* that Reg looks uglier than a fish.'

'I'm so very, very sorry,' said Peter, his voice level and bland.

'In any case,' said Toby, 'food doesn't have to be fancy to be good.'

This meant that the conversation drifted unpleasantly on to whether or not money makes you a better person.

Peter was really stupid about it all. 'I would rather die than be poor,' was one arrogant and irritating thing he spouted. 'I bet you don't get paid much,' he also said, speaking to Toby, who somehow kept his cool, even though Jason laughed a little.

Lee was almost as mad in the opposite direction, saying that rich people should be put in prison and have their possessions taken away by the government.

Matt sat between the two. 'Hey, man; hey, man,' he

said, looking one way and then the other. 'It doesn't matter how much money someone has, so long as he's a dude.' I agreed. But Matt's charm, so effective on me and Reg, and perhaps Luke and Alastair, didn't work at all on the others.

A slightly bad feeling hung over lunch. I chatted to Toby in as friendly a way as possible, so did Matt: Toby must have been annoyed by what had been said. But he was so even-tempered nothing seemed to get to him.

In the afternoon there were three more activities, but this time a man called Rob came in to take the sessions (he had been with the girls in the morning). It was hard to tell how old Rob was – his face was like a walnut from so much sun.

The first lesson was tracking. Rob was so good at this I couldn't believe it wasn't a set-up. He showed us how to follow animal tracks by looking for *spoor*. We were all a bit sceptical about this, given that one broken twig looks the same as another, and testing the temperature of animal poo to tell how far away the creature is seems crazy. But he then asked for a volunteer, and Luke was told to run off through the thick bushes behind the house. We were spellbound as Rob tracked him down – it was like something out of *Lord of the Rings*.

'I can't believe you did that,' squealed Luke as he was discovered curled up inside a bush.

'You can run, but you can't hide,' said Jason.

Peter was the only person who was any good at tracking, apart from Toby and Jason, who had done it a hundred times. It's strange how sometimes a person has unexpected skills.

Next, Rob did a session on rope-making. It was enough to leave most people bored, but Matt and I gabbled away while sorting out the twines and forgot about everyone else.

Finally, Rob did a session on knife skills. This wasn't a very successful session. The most significant thing was that Alastair refused to handle a knife; in fact, he pretty much refused to be within sight of one. It was a serious phobia.

'But what about knives at the dinner table?' asked Jason. 'Are you scared by them?'

'Different.' Alastair turned quickly and walked off to the house.

'What's with him?' asked Peter.

'He was attacked on a London street about a year ago,' said Jason. '*Another* troubled kid sent on this trip to get better.'

Peter stretched and yawned. 'Yeah. This trip doesn't seem to attract normal people. Apart from me, of course.'

I distinctly remember Lee's comment: 'Anyway, nothing wrong with knives. One of the best and most interesting ways to kill someone.'

It was in the early evening that Luke fell ill. You all know that he died three days later, but this was when it all started. It was a sudden decline, but we had no idea, not the faintest clue, how serious it was.

At about seven o'clock he complained of feeling really tired and dizzy, but still had his Luke-ish ways, trying to make the best of it. But he was shivering and said he felt sick. At eight o'clock he threw up on the beach and made a mess in his trousers. It was pretty bad. He then went to bed.

Importantly, just after 9.30 p.m., he felt hungry and ate some soup.

After that, probably fatally, he was encouraged to sip water as often as possible.

I'm now fairly sure both the soup and the water were poisoned, but we all thought it was just a stomach bug or some sort of flu. To be honest, we wondered if Luke was just making a bit of a fuss over nothing.

Yes, I was the one who took him the soup at 9.35 p.m. – I've explained below how I remember the time. I collected the bowl from Toby in the kitchen, carried it to the room and left it on the little table that had been put in his room. [I DID NOTHING ELSE. I didn't add anything, not even a drop of water, and simply carried the soup directly into the room. I didn't leave the soup anywhere else. It's as simple as that.]

I stayed for a few minutes and spoke briefly to Luke. He was holding his stomach and wincing, but that didn't stop him apologizing a few times, which I took as being about the illness, because it was a bit of a nuisance. 'If you feel better, you're very welcome to come down on the rocks with me and Matt,' I said.

'I don't think I'll be doing that,' Luke said quietly. 'I'm sorry. I *am* sorry. Really I am.'

It seemed logical that he should just sleep it off.

'Make sure you drink plenty of water,' I said. I wish I hadn't, but it was what people *always* say to someone who is unwell. The thought of poisonous black bean or *Castanospermum australe* seeds being ground into water and on to food to infect it (supposing the police are right about how it was done) never entered my head.

We were more interested in what was going on

outside – at the time, Luke's illness was a side-issue compared to the presence of Zara and Belle. On the first night we had been in the middle of the group, right next to the house; on the second night we were down on the beach, separated from the others; on this third night we went a little way round the bay and on to some rocks. When night came, the others were distant in a bubble of light by the house. We felt peaceful in the darkness, with nothing more than the torches on our phones to see by.

What did we talk about? Everything and nothing. Some of it was serious and some of it was stupid. Matt was on the form of his life, and I did feel a tiny bit excluded when both girls were so wrapped up in his witty chat, staring at him when he spoke, but he had the same effect on me.

You see, how could I possibly have been scheming about killing Luke, who I really liked, when I was enjoying the best part of a disastrous holiday?

It was at 9.20 p.m. (I remember looking) by my digital watch when I offered to walk up to the house and get us some more food. Zara said that she would come with me, and we talked on the way about match-making Matt and Belle.

Nick, Peter, Lee and Jason were sitting outside the door

that led to the beach when we arrived and said we were after a bit more of the barbecued stuff.

'I've just taken in what's left,' said Jason. 'You'll have to raid the kitchen.'

'There's a sausage waiting for you inside, Zara,' said Peter.

Nick spluttered, excessively, as always. He didn't seem to mind being Peter's follower.

I was surprised that Lee joined in. 'Have you been between a rock and a hard place?'

Zara was really composed. She stopped, looked each one in the eye while they sat there gormlessly, and sweetly said: 'Can we hurry up, George? I find it hard to keep my hands off you.'

Their mouths popped open and shut like goldfish.

'If you want to research, I suggest you look on the internet,' she concluded.

I could see that they all hated me for not having to say a word.

We walked through to the kitchen where Toby and Andrea were clearing up and pouring some soup into a bowl for Luke.

'I'll drop that off with the plague victim,' I offered.

Toby therefore wrote the now notorious line in the

medical report: *George Fleet took soup mid-eve and chatted to Luke.*

Actually, I didn't say much to Luke, and at the time I didn't understand much of what he said to me. It was like we were having separate conversations, but I just thought it was the fever talking.

I asked Luke how he felt.

'I had to do it,' he whispered.

I said that I knew he would be fine.

'I just didn't want to be hit again,' he said.

I know I made a *huge* mistake – probably the biggest of the trip (and my life?). If only I'd been less worried about getting back to the beach with Zara and more worried about what Luke was talking about, I could have stopped everything in its tracks. But I didn't imagine things had been going on that I was ignorant of. I didn't know that Luke was a victim of both poison and serious intimidation.

So I left, saying, 'You'll feel better in the morning. You're just confused by the bug. Try to sleep.'

I can be a selfish bastard sometimes and I feel really guilty about it.

We were on the beach after that for about another ninety minutes. We had moved on to Spin the Bottle – it felt like a game we'd all left behind years ago, and that made it even more fun – before Andrea called out for the girls.

As we were going, Zara stopped and looked me in the eye. 'Thanks for a great evening.'

As I walked away I thought of Jess.

Inside, Luke was worse. His breathing wasn't good and he threw up every now and again, just small amounts. We trooped in and out of the doorway to his room, wishing him well, imagining that amount of distance would protect us from infection, little knowing there was no virus to be caught.

'You'll be fine in the morning,' Jason said. 'If you're not better, we'll call the doc.'

But Luke wasn't better in the morning.

[Here ends the ninth part of George's statement]

135

THE OTHER CHAPTER 9
(SAID IN THE HOUR BEFORE):
HIM

No one feels sorry when a WORM dies.

No one cries when a fly is SQUASHED. (No one *normal*.)

Millions of people EAT dead animals. Including YOU.

Admit it, not even YOU feel bad about swatting a wasp, and you think you're all so holy and perfect, and a never-do-anything-wrong-in-a-million-years type of person.

Why is it that everyone thinks that they're the good guy and everyone else is wrong? Even little people like you think like that. It's **pathetic**.

Luke should have realized what it meant to be a pupil . A PUPIL takes orders from his MASTER. He should worship his master, especially if his master is a GENIUS.

A pupil who FAILS his master is guilty of TREASON.

Those guilty of *treason* should be punished with DEATH.

I will admit to YOU, in the spirit of friendship and love and kindness, despite hating you more than I hate something stuck to my shoe that has been walked into the house and up the stairs in stinking brown blobs, that I was a bit slow to see the opportunity of that boring session on plants.

But.

Castanospermum australe – that's the name. Black bean.
Cast-a-no-<u>sperm</u>-um. Beans.

Poisonous beans.

Beans, beans, good for the heart.

Very tasty for lunch and supper.

You know what my favourite Chinese dish is? Yep.
Chicken in black bean sauce. I love those little black specks.
Yum yum – I lick my lips.

Sorry to mention this if you're hungry. You must be
hungry. And thirsty. Would you like some of this water?

[Pause]

Be careful.

Maybe it's poisoned.

[Pause]

Best pour it away. The earth is dry and thirsty. Its
desperate for it. See how quickly it drinks.

[Pause]

It wasn't poisoned.

I lied.

[Pause]

YOU SEE WHAT YOU ARE DEALING WITH.

EVIDENCE #2

EMAIL FROM LUKE BERTRAND TO
HIS LEGAL GUARDIAN

Hi Nan,

I'm a bit out of it tonite – must've eaten something I shouldn't've off the barbie.

Having a good time, tho. There's so much happening.

Someone here knows about what happened before I came to live with you, so I did something to that George boy, and shouldn't have. I don't feel good about that, especially because he was in here as if it didn't matter, getting me to look after myself. He's good.

But I don't feel too good, so will go off to nod, as you would say.

I'll be better in the morn, I'm sure.

Give my love to Gramps and a big woof to Bertie.

Lots of love,

Lukey

As this was the final day at the beach, and we were travelling from late afternoon, while we ate breakfast Toby reminded us what was going to happen next. The Ultimate Bushcraft Gold Star Challenge was a six-day hike between two very remote points on Cape York, starting and finishing with a long minibus drive.

'It's all very simple despite being in the middle of one of the most remote places on the planet,' said Toby. 'Nowhere is more than ten miles from a shelter with communication and provisions, but it's highly unlikely we will bump into anyone. And if anything goes wrong we'll radio for help and the doc will 'copter in and have you back in Cairns within the hour.'

'It's a picnic,' said Jason. 'The girls are doing a similar course, starting about twenty miles from us.' He smirked. 'If they can do it, I'm sure that even you lot can.'

'Jase and I carry satellite phones and UHF radios, and the overnight cabins all have radio communication,' said Toby. 'You'll each have a personal locator beacon – and a walkie-talkie.'

'Yeah – a walkie-talkie and a beacon, bring it on,' Nick mumbled sarcastically.

Toby ignored him: 'Jase and I are both trained with the old-fashioned map and compass, but we know the route pretty well already. That's it – all sorted. It's one of the most wickedly on-the-edge things you'll ever do in your life.'

'Has anyone ever hurt themselves?' asked Lee.

'We've had all sorts of serious injuries in the past,' Jason said. 'A stubbed toe, a grazed knee, a bit of indigestion. You'll live.'

'Where do we use the toilet?' asked Reg.

'Behind a bush, numbskull,' said Nick. 'There's about a *billion* bushes. Even you'll be hidden.'

'Guys, really,' Toby added, 'everything has been carefully thought about to be totally exciting but absolutely safe. It's awesome.'

Everyone showed some excitement – a murmur or a whoop depending on who they were. I had an idea of a landscape of wooded hills and craggy valleys that didn't turn out to be far from the truth.

Luke's condition wasn't helped because it was unusually hot for the time of year. It was in the morning that the doctor came to see him, but you can't blame the doctor for failing to spot that Luke had been poisoned. Who would have imagined that? It was more mess-up than conspiracy, I'm sure.

One part of the story I'm properly ashamed about happened halfway through the last day of training, just after lunch. I'm ashamed because it was something that was out of character.

The day was all about teamwork and building – in particular, building a sort of treehouse, though Jason said that some past achievements (of which some evidence remained) had been little more than a few logs leaning against a tree to form a basic shelter.

Matt and I were now an obvious pair and put to work alongside Al and Reg. That left Nick, Peter and Lee in the other 'four' – given that Luke was inside, getting further and further from a point of rescue. It was a sort of competition. The girls were doing the same thing on the same day, and that made it a competition between the sexes as well.

We were working on the outcrop of land to the right of the bay in a roughly parallel position to the girls to the left of the bay. The other group of boys was out of sight – it was part of the game that we had to find our own design.

141

I was chopping wood when a splinter shot out and stabbed me on an unprotected bit of my arm. Matt insisted on being my saviour and pulling out the chip; it came out cleanly and quickly, but was followed by blood, which spilt out down my arm and on to my shorts and T-shirt. It wasn't exactly a flood, but it was too much to ignore. Toby gave me a plaster, but the blood was soon fighting its way through, turning the plaster into a dark red, damp smudge, and the same thing happened to a second plaster – it was only on the third that it stopped. By then it was clear that I would have to go back to the house and change clothes. Bloody fingerprints had got everywhere.

I was fine and have never had a problem with blood, whether my own or others', so was more annoyed with wasting time (and messing my favourite T-shirt) than worried about the injury – which was, in any case, soon forgotten.

There were two ways back to the house. One was through the trees near to the other group, which was bound to lead to accusations of cheating; the other way was next to the shore. The latter had the advantage of being in sight of the girls and I heard a few shouts as I jogged that way. I waved, trying to look braver and more injured than I actually was.

I arrived at the house and changed. I was just leaving when Zara appeared out of the woods on the far side.

'Are you OK?' she said. 'I said I'd come to check on you.'

I said that I was fine, that it was only a scratch, but then held my arm in a way that suggested it was in danger of amputation.

'Let me have a look,' she said.

We sat down on the wooden step at the edge of the house and she gently pressed the area with her finger. Her hair brushed my neck and I looked down at her bare legs. Then she angled round and I looked at her face. I moved my head forward a bit and she responded. Almost immediately we were kissing. Her fingers touched my cheek. I then said – and I still can't believe I said this – 'Would you like to go inside?'

She nodded. 'Yes.' She stood up and took my hand.

You must think I'm really untrustworthy – but I was just stupid. I was thousands of miles away from Jess and it was a totally different sunny world, and we were on holiday, and . . .

We went into my room and locked the door.

When it was over, I looked up to the window and there, just for about one second, was a blur of movement.

Someone had seen everything – or at least enough to know what was going on.

'There was someone there,' I said to Zara, awkwardly standing up and adjusting my clothes. I was already feeling irresponsible and stupid. I thought of Jess and felt depressed. 'I'm sure I saw something.'

'I didn't see anyone,' Zara said. Her eyes avoided mine, but she briefly put her hand on my chest. 'This'll be our secret.' Then she unlocked the door. 'But we should get back to our teams . . .'

I opened the window to see who was there, but saw no one.

Just then, the door burst open and Matt flew in. 'How's it going?' He raised his eyebrows. 'What are you two up to? Keeping the British end up?'

'Um, er, did you see someone outside?' I stammered.

'We're all outside, you dingo,' said Matt. 'It's sweltering, so we came back for a drink.' He turned to Zara. 'Andrea's looking for you. 'Old on – what *were* you doing in here? I hope I haven't interrupted something.'

Zara's face reddened and she pointed to my injured arm. 'Just sorting this.'

'OK – Doctors and Nurses!' he chuckled, before walking off down the corridor and singing to himself.

Zara and I followed Matt outside and wandered towards the group. There were a few comments about what we'd been up to, but I doubt anyone *actually* thought it was true – anyone apart from the person who had seen us. At the time I didn't know who it was, of course, but now I can remember how he was turned away from the rest of the group. *Now* I know he was eaten up by disgust and anger.

We quickly added the finishing touches to our shelters before we visited each one in turn, analysing stability and usefulness. The girls were still with us. The theory was that we'd give each one a mark out of ten, but it turned into a competition of who could find the most original/absurd/sexist criticism of the other's efforts. Both girls' groups had cheated, we thought, by using plastic sheeting as a cover – plastic wouldn't be available in the wilderness.

I barely joined in and didn't say much when the girls left. I was feeling bad because Jess had sent me a slushy text while I was inside with Zara. But on our way back up to the house I began to shake off the guilt – downplaying it in my mind – mainly because of Matt's joking around, which distracted me.

Reg joined in our increasingly stupid conversation, and Alastair listened. Nick, Peter and Lee slouched off to one side, just out of earshot, full of disdain, muttering to one another and sneering. This separation had become the norm. Usually they were hanging around Jason, but I suppose it's true that Matt, Reg and I were usually with Toby. Alastair was the one person who moved between the groups, not quite fitting in with either.

We then packed one rucksack each for the big hike. To keep down weight, it was a case of taking the absolute minimum. 'No room for luxuries,' Toby said. We anticipated being back after the hike for three days of genuine rest and relaxation.

I was surprised by how thin Luke looked, and how he didn't get out of bed to see us off. I said something like, 'Bye, Luke, see you later,' but he didn't reply. I am angry with myself for not having done more – but I simply didn't understand then. I was distracted by stupid ordinary things like getting my bag on the bus.

Jason stayed with Luke while a driver took the rest of us in the loaded-up minibus on the short trip to the girls' house. When we were about halfway there, we had to pull to one side of the unevenly tarmacked track to let another car go by. Toby said it was the Ultimate Bushcraft person who was going to look after Luke and watch him till the doctor came back the following morning. Soon after, Jason came jogging through the trees to rejoin us.

We all suspected that the real reason for stopping off was so that Toby could say goodbye to Andrea, but it meant that at about 4 p.m. we had a quick meeting to say farewell to the girls.

'Come on,' said Matt as he strode towards Belle, 'let's move in on the totty.'

I felt uneasy and held back a bit.

'Not going to say goodbye to your girlfriend?' said Peter. 'Or did you do that earlier?'

I went forward to Zara, which wasn't easy in front of everyone. 'See you at the halfway point.' I smiled as she met my eye and winked.

'Yeah,' she said. 'Race you there. Just shout if you get lost and we'll come and rescue you.'

[I know that you have access to the report about how Luke died from complications caused by poisoning two days later. We all know that if Luke had seen a doctor again that evening instead of the next morning, and got to hospital sooner, he might have been saved. Cairns Hospital immediately placed Luke in their Intensive Care Unit as soon as he was rushed through the doors by the air ambulance team. They were brilliant and did everything possible to save him. No one can be blamed apart from the poisoner. But it took another twenty-four hours before the doctors understood that there had been a murder, and by then things had moved on quickly.]

To get to the start of the hike we drove past lots of isolated places, getting more distant from civilization by the minute. I sat next to Matt, of course. Jason was at the back next to Peter, rather than up front next to Toby. Reg was behind me (again), his knees jabbing into my back, but I said nothing.

At just past 5 p.m. we turned into a lane with little tracks running off it – and finally, after more than four hours in total, we stopped on a ridge at the end of a barely driveable trail. There was a fairly large wooden hut, something like a chalet, waiting for us at the end of it.

It was dark when we arrived.

'This is almost certainly the most isolated you've ever been while on land,' Jason said enthusiastically, his elbow resting on Peter's shoulder. 'The nearest human life, the girls, is about twenty-five miles that way.' He pointed vaguely into the dark.

Before the minibus left us there was an equipment check. I heard Toby contact the Rangers' Office at the Staaten River National Park and then speak to someone else, probably Andrea. Less than five minutes later the minibus went trundling back down the hill, bouncing into dips and round rocks as it went, leaving us alone in the wilderness.

'Gather together, guys,' Toby said. He was holding something up. 'This is our lifeline – it's a satellite phone and the only thing that will get a good signal out here. If I suddenly disappear, and Jason suddenly disappears, you have to dial 000 and give the location on *this* device.' He held up a personal locator beacon in his other hand. 'You'll all be given one of these before we set off tomorrow. Just reel off the numbers *here*. If the phone vaporizes, this thing on my belt is an ultra-high-frequency radio, and that'll also reach the nearest ranger, as well as the girls' group.'

There were no questions. No one was interested in the safety stuff.

'On the way, each night we stop at a hut numbered one through to six. Inside is yet *another* radio.' He reached down and picked a walkie-talkie out of a plastic box. 'These are vital within the group. They have a range of about ten miles. That means you can always contact the nearest hut.'

Still no questions. Even I was zoning out (and I can't swear to exactly what Toby said).

'And make the most of this hut. It's *by far* the most luxurious. Some of the others are just one room. Even though it's hot, you don't want to sleep outside with the beasties unless you're totally secure inside a tent. Now – the next few days will create memories you'll have for the rest of your life. So make it count, boys!'

'Will the animals come near us in the night?' said Reg.

There was laughter and a few comments.

'Nothing wild will be feasting on you if you keep inside or zip up your tent,' said Jason. We knew that we would be in tents when we reached huts one and five, which were sheds in the middle of nowhere.

'There are no big creatures,' Toby reassured us, 'apart from crocs, and they'll only be near the water, if you catch a glimpse of any at all. But avoid snakes and toads – and spiders, of course. There're a few funnel-webs scuttling around in some parts of Oz looking for prime pommy flesh.'

It felt like a genuine adventure with just enough danger to be exciting. We made a fire and I ate some sausages and chunks of steak, and then settled down in a room with Matt, Reg and Alastair. Shattered, and despite fears of scorpions (though we had been told that the Aussie scorpion wasn't that dangerous), I fell asleep immediately.

I'm a deep sleeper and didn't hear anything all night. The next morning, the first official day of the hike, everything had been turned upside down.

[Here ends the tenth part of George's statement]

THE OTHER CHAPTER 10
(SAID IN THE HOUR BEFORE):
HIM

Remember the final day before we went into the WILDerness?

I need to STAY CALM while we talk about this one.

It should've been a happy day with Luke slipping away while everyone went on about flu. He was A SLAVE rather than a pupil. He had FAILED. And he would have told *sooner* or *later*. He was beginning to get a bit independent – a bit less fearful.

<u>Lack</u> of fear is a terrible mistake.

Remember that. Remember that while you're with me.

THIS'LL MAKE HIM BETTER . . .

OH YES IT WILL.

OH NO IT WON'T!

You probably wonder what pushed me over the edge – what made me do this.

Oooooooooh – it's just that he's bad. A *very naughty boy*.

I'm a very naughty boy. I should HIT MYSELF.

. . .

I'm JOKING.

Remember how superior I AM.

ONE thing led to ANOTHER. Matt on the plane – that was just a laugh.

THEN: GEORGEY, my opposite. Goody-goody caught up in his own stupid obsession with himself and being as perfect as a totally blank sheet of paper.

One thing led to another.

THAT'S LIFE.

THAT'S DEATH.

<u>**TWO THINGS**</u>:

Just wait as I get my thoughts together.

HA! Don't go wandering off.

ONE:

You won't understand because you're really stupid and don't know what day of the week it is and just sit there covered in BLOOD and SPIT.

You're too thick to understand how REPULSIVE it was to see everyone sucking up to you.

TWO:

I was *lucky*.

Lucky to have found Luke; AND even *luckier* to have found a proper servant.

Now.

Listen carefully.

I will speak nice and quietly for you.

Was it *luck*?

NO.

It was MY GENIUS.

. . .

It worries me that you're so THICK IN THE HEAD that you can't work out who my assistant is.

How about we turn it into a game?

YOU have to work out who has helped me, and if you guess correctly <u>first</u> time, I'll let you go.

But if you're wrong – then, OH DEAR, it's the chop for you.

THUMP.

STATEMENT #8

HAMISH TATE, CEO OF THE
ULTIMATE BUSHCRAFT COMPANY

At all times, a reasonable duty of care was shown by Toby Jones regarding the boys on the trip in question. This is a statement of fact, not to protect the memory of someone sadly no longer with us.

Boys are not hospitalized for sickness – that is not reasonable. Neither should every illness be investigated for poison. Hindsight is a fine thing. Toby Jones was a decent young man with a great future ahead of him. May he rest in peace.

The Ultimate Bushcraft Company cannot reasonably protect against the sort of cunning psychopath responsible for these crimes.

The trip, I remind you, left with more than the required hardware: two satellite phones, two UHF radios, local communication devices, a full set of PLBs [Personal Locator Beacons], and, in Toby Jones, a highly trained and trusted group leader.

I woke with a start.

'When we find Toby, he'll sort it out,' were the first words I heard in Jason's heavy Australian twang.

Before I had a chance to talk to the others, Nick was in the room. 'Have you got Toby and Peter in here?' He looked at me dismissively. 'I know you don't let Toby out of your sight.'

'What's going on, man?' said Alastair.

'Toby and Peter have gone walkabout and there's a problem with the radio. Come on, don't just lie there,' said Nick.

We threw clothes on and went into the main room, a kitchen, which the three bedrooms and toilet opened into. Toby and Peter were nowhere to be seen.

'What's the soap opera?' said Matt.

Nick was looking at the back of the cabin radio.

'Those bastards,' said Nick. 'I bet this is part of a game Toby is playing and they think this is all a big [words edited] laugh.' He spun the radio round. All the wires had

156

been cut – sliced cleanly with a knife or scissors. 'It's just a piece of junk now.'

'What about the satellite phones?' I said.

'Are you blind? This one is Jason's.' Nick held it up – the wires had also been wrenched out of the back. 'It was left here last night and some joker has arsed around with it. Where the hell is that idiot, Toby?'

'There's no way Toby would do this for a joke,' I said to Nick.

Jason strode in and emptied a box of personal locator beacons on to the table in the middle of the room. 'Some git has taken all the batteries out. They were definitely there last night. I saw them myself.'

None of it computed. 'We've got to find Toby,' I said.

'No kidding, Sherlock,' said Lee sarcastically. 'You're a real genius. I *think* that might be a good idea.'

'Toby this, Toby that, I love Toby, let me get in his pants,' taunted Nick, staring at me.

Jason then opened the box of walkie-talkies. He tried two at random: both switched on to static, then he blew into one and a rushing wind sound came out of the other. 'Great,' he said. 'These are working fine. Take one each.'

It was a beautifully sunny day – as they all were. We were on a thumb-shaped outcrop of land with a sweeping wooded valley in front of us to the north. The path we were meant to follow was to the west, down a gentle slope. To the north and east there was a much sharper drop, pretty much a cliff, with large boulders at the bottom. Behind us the land fell slightly and was covered in trees. Matt and I wandered aimlessly in that direction, down the track the minibus had taken the previous night, mainly because the others headed the opposite way.

Then came one of those dreadful everything-changes moments. We saw Alastair return to the hut, panting furiously, pointing, then running back in the direction he had come from. Matt and I hurtled after him; shouts went out to the others.

A little way round the crown of the hill towards the east, still on the fairly narrow path, Alastair stopped and pointed down towards the large boulders at the bottom. There were bodies down there.

There was a thick bush to the side of the path that had been squashed and snapped, and there were scuff marks across the track to the cliff edge. It looked like there had been a fight, then a fall.

'Right,' said Jason. 'Everyone's to stay here. No questions. I'm going to investigate.'

It was impossible to go straight down – it was sheer to

begin with, and then sheer again after a ledge that hadn't been wide enough to break their fall. Jason had to go back past the hut and then down a much longer route. About fifteen minutes later we saw him picking his way over the rocks towards the bodies.

We held our breath as he disappeared behind the boulder. We could see Peter's distinctive red-and-black trainers. Jason stood up and shook his head.

'Oh my God,' I muttered. Despite all the evidence, I still wanted to believe it was an awful accident. We stared, silenced by the horror of it all.

Jason then went across a few boulders to the second body: even though it was blood-splattered and broken, it was unmistakably Toby.

I found myself saying *oh no* repeatedly, stupidly, unable to unfreeze my brain. Others shouted and swore over and over again. Although I'd only known them for a few days, I had a real sense of loss.

'Go back to the hut and stay inside,' hollered Jason.

We were slow to do that. Like cattle or sheep, we drifted back as a helpless flock.

You might think that we stayed like that for hours, but it's not like that in real life. People soon realize that they're not the one who is dead – and no one can imagine himself

159

dying. It's always *others*. And we didn't realize the extent of the danger. We didn't know about Luke, of course. It must be hard for you to understand. None of it seemed real – it was as if there was going to be a sudden and obvious explanation that meant Toby and Peter weren't dead after all.

Toby. Dead. He would have gone on to do fantastic things. He was a great person. He was the sort of person I would like to be. And Peter. Peter was too young to die.

But soon we were exchanging theories about what had happened. To be honest: concern about ourselves shoved out worry about the dead. 'Could Peter have got in trouble and Toby fell trying to save him?' suggested Matt. 'Toby would be brave if he had to be.'

'Maybe Toby attacked and killed Peter and then, filled with guilt at his *vile* crime and assault, jumped himself?' That was Nick. 'Peter was all right. Toby was probably jealous. Or he had other secret twisted reasons for attacking him.'

'You really are full of shit,' I said to him.

'Yeah?' Nick replied, pushing me. 'Yeah?' Another shove. 'Be careful that you don't slip as well. We don't want any more *weirdos* to die.' He didn't actually punch me, but his shoulder and arm made firm contact with mine.

Matt got between us, as did Lee.

'Come on,' said Lee. 'We need to pull together. Fighting amongst ourselves won't help.' Then he added quietly: 'The evidence would suggest that there's been enough of that already.'

Nick and I both took a step away from one another, but if either of us had flinched, it would have started again, but worse. I think I hated him at this point, but not badly enough to want to really hurt him.

'You need to watch yourself,' Nick said to me as he stalked off, pushing away Lee's arm.

We had just made it back into the cabin when Jason returned. 'Look,' he said, straight away, with no introduction. 'They're both dead, and at this stage there's no point asking how or why. We just need to get help as soon as we can, especially as Toby's satellite phone is nowhere to be seen – probably smashed to bits on a rock – just as his radio was.'

There was more swearing and muttering.

'How long before someone comes to get us?' said Alastair.

'They'll probably be concerned if we don't check in

tonight, but it could be forty-eight hours. I don't know, do I? Nothing like this has ever happened before. But I don't think we should sit here while those bodies go bad in the heat and get eaten by animals.'

Reg said that he felt sick.

Jason ignored him: 'The next hut is about twelve miles away. We should do the walk as planned and radio from there.'

'I think it's more sensible to stay put,' said Alastair, who was still examining the radio, probably hoping to get it going again. 'They know we're here, and this is where they'll start looking.'

'Except they *don't* know we're here. They think we're out there.' Jason waved his arm vaguely. 'If anything, they'll be expecting us at the second camp by this evening.'

'Do we *all* have to go?' asked Reg tearfully. 'I don't like this. There could be anyone or any*thing* out there.'

Jason slammed his fist down on to the table. 'Don't be so *weak*. This isn't a horror movie. Yeah, we do all have to go.' He glared at Reg and then the rest of us. 'Let me be [word deleted] blunt about two things. The first is that I'm in charge and you little [word deleted] are going to let me sort this out. And, second, I'm worried that we're not alone out here.' He looked at the windows. 'We need to stick together.'

'I think Jason's right,' I said. 'We need to get help as soon as possible, and that means going to the nearest radio as soon as we can.'

'Georgey is right. I'll go if Georgey goes,' said Reg, now crying properly and hugging himself. He looked at me for reassurance and I nodded.

'Blah! Blah! Blah!' said Nick. 'How pathetic. It's just a little wander through some trees. I say we'll find there was more to Toby than we thought.' Nick jabbed his finger at me. 'He always looked at the blond one here in a weird way. Let's get this walk done.'

How did I feel about Nick now that I had calmed down? I was angry that he didn't show *any* respect for the dead. Not even for his so-called friend, Peter.

Jason then told us to pack immediately – we would be off in ten minutes.

Matt was shivering slightly but tried to make light of it. 'I wish we had a carrier pigeon. Maybe we could send a smoke signal?'

This gave me the idea to leave a note in the cabin, explaining what had happened and calling for help. I took a pencil from the kitchen, tore the back page from a book that had been left in the front of my rucksack and sat on my bunk to write:

FOLLOWING THE DEATHS OF TOBY AND PETER, WE ARE WALKING ON TO THE SECOND CABIN. THEIR BODIES ARE TO THE EAST OF HERE AT THE BOTTOM OF THE DROP. WE HAVE NO WAY OF COMMUNICATION OTHER THAN THE WALKIE-TALKIES. PLEASE SEND HELP URGENTLY.

- GEORGE FLEET ON BEHALF OF THE GROUP

I went into the kitchen, rolled up the note, poked it into an old plastic water bottle so half of it was poking out and left it in the middle of the table.

Lee was standing on the other side of the table and showed with a nod of his head that he wanted me to go outside. Everyone else was still in their room packing. I dropped my rucksack by the door and followed.

We stood exactly where the minibus had stopped the previous evening, just beyond the hearing of the others.

'I don't like this,' Lee whispered.

'Have you *really* called me out here to say that?' I said.

'Yes,' he continued, leaning forward. 'I don't like this *logically*.' He adjusted his glasses and then put his hands on his hips. 'Let's say Toby wanted to kill Peter for some weird reason, but then felt guilty about it and committed suicide.'

164

I began to protest. 'But we know that Toby wasn't like that . . .'

'I know,' said Lee. 'But just suppose. Or suppose that he tried to grab Peter, who then dragged Toby over the edge with him. In either case, why would Toby destroy most of the communication devices first? Why make us walk to the next hut? And why sabotage the location devices? It doesn't achieve anything.' He looked back at the hut. 'And supposing Toby is victim rather than attacker. There's no one here strong enough to drag him out there and kill him. Not even Nick could do that. Nick and you together? Possibly. But Toby would have made one hell of a noise and woken us all up. And why also kill Peter? I don't like this one bit.' He glanced around. 'In my view, we are not alone.' He strode back into the hut, his voice trailing off.

I was left out there – my head spinning with frightened thoughts. I looked at the surrounding trees, half expecting to see eyes.

'Come on, Georgey,' said Jason from the door of the hut. 'It's time.'

I returned to collect my rucksack, which was just inside the door, exactly where I'd left it. As I hauled it on to my shoulders, I noticed that the table was empty. 'I left something on the table,' I said to no one in particular.

Matt was coming out of the room we had slept in. 'Lost something?'

'I put something on the table,' I repeated, pointing. 'A message in a bottle.'

'Well, there's nothing there now,' said Nick from outside. 'Stop arsing around. Don't you know that two people are dead?'

'But . . .' Something stopped me from saying more. I had been thinking that there was an accidental or absurd reason for the deaths, but this jabbed serious doubt into my mind. It was the very first time I considered that my near-accident when climbing, Luke's illness, maybe even Matt's allergic reaction on the plane, and what was happening now were all connected. I feared that meant someone seriously evil was inside the group. I immediately thought of Nick: he had the physical strength – and probably the character – to do something hideous. 'Keep an eye on Nick,' I whispered to Matt as he passed. 'I don't trust him.'

Matt was pale with anxiety. 'OK, mate. Yeah, OK. Let's stick close.'

We gathered in a circle outside.

'Boys,' said Jason. 'Now that Toby isn't with us, it's my job to get you to the second hut.' He waved the map.

'I've done this before and it's the easiest route of the week. Everything will soon be over. I'll take care of everything.'

It was a fairly straightforward walk – to begin with, we were basically heading down one slope, across a valley and up the other side – but it would have been difficult without Jason's maps and compass. He had two maps: one was a fairly standard OS-style Geography-lesson map, and the other was marked with a very detailed description of the route to take: *after going down the slope bear NE for about 500 metres along the bank of a stream (perhaps dry at some times of the year)* – that sort of thing. I probably could have found my way on my own with this guidance.

We walked in near silence and single file. Jason was first, followed by Nick. I wanted to keep an eye on everyone, especially Nick, so went last with Matt in front of me.

Reg, suffering badly in the heat, his clothes soaked in sweat, was in front of Matt. He sometimes fell back until he was close to me.

I quietly told him that everything would be OK. I still thought it would be. 'This'll be over soon. We just need to be brave,' I said each time.

After maybe five or six miles we had climbed up the other side of the valley and now stood on the ridge. All around us was really colourful landscape. Birds flapped nearby and there was the hum of the jungle. There was no sign of anyone else.

It was hot, so Jason said we should stop for lunch. 'The hut is over there on the hills, about two or three hours away,' he explained. The terrain was more complicated and uneven – often thick with trees, but with some open bits.

We spread ourselves out and nibbled at crackers and cheese and apples. I don't think anyone was very hungry, but we drank lots. I walked off to go to the toilet and looked over to the east, wondering about the girls. Flicking through the different channel settings on the walkie-talkie, I spoke into each one: 'Is anyone there?'

Channel 19: 'Is anyone there?' (Wait. Nothing.)

Channel 20: 'Is anyone there?' (Wait. Nothing.)

Channel 21: 'Is anyone there?'

There was a moment of fuzzy cracking, and I was about to try the next channel – but then, fizzing and indistinct: 'Is that you?' More crackling, then: 'I've sorted it.'

I should have played it cleverly, but was surprised and excited, my sweaty hands slipping on the walkie-talkie. 'Who is it?' I gabbled. 'Can you help us?'

There was nothing more, just uninterrupted dull static.

'Come in!' I said, my lips brushing the microphone. 'Come in!'

I jogged back to the group and found Matt walking towards me. 'Have you been on the radio? I thought I might have heard something. Channel twenty-one?' I asked.

'No,' he replied. 'I've been on channel nine – the one Jason told us to use.'

I was about to say what I'd heard when my brain started to work. *I've sorted it.* I didn't like it. I've *sorted* it.

I swore, but hoped I was over-thinking it. 'Is everyone else OK?'

'Yeah. I think we're going to be—'

The sound that interrupted Matt wasn't exactly a scream – it was something from nearer the back of the throat, terror and pain at once, a caveman's cry rather than a shout.

The noise came again, even more urgent, louder, more chilling. It was the sound of someone who had completely lost it.

Matt and I ran back to the others. Jason was the first person we saw. He looked like he was about to crack. 'Who's making that noise? Where's it coming from?' he yelled.

With Jason and Matt, I jogged in the general direction of the noise, half hoping that we would hear it again and

169

be able to follow it, but half hoping there would be no more of it. Others came into view, now converging on us. I saw Nick and Lee. Then there was Alastair.

Reg was missing. 'Reg?' I shouted. 'Reg!'

There was another noise, the same urgency, but much quieter and closer. Desperate.

I sprinted, and there was Reg, face down on the ground, hands tied behind his back. He had thrown up, and had something like foam coming out of his mouth. He was trying to wriggle but didn't have the strength. I didn't have time to think. Ignoring the mess, I leant down and started to fumble with the cord around his wrists – it was an untidy but secure knot. 'You're safe now,' I said, still fighting with the knot. 'What happened?'

The others stood staring, doing nothing.

Reg continued to shiver. 'Get it away,' he whispered, and then, quickly: 'He-did-it.' He was starting to shake.

'Talk to me, Reg, talk to me,' I screeched as the others gathered closer.

The knot had come free, but Reg still didn't move properly. He looked up, pleading in one breath: 'Geddidout.'

I suddenly noticed that there was something moving under his shirt and shorts. I leapt back in shock, briefly grabbing a piece of Reg's shirt between my finger and thumb as I fell on my back and then pushed myself up in one desperate movement.

Moving quickly and erratically, a spider scuttled free. It was black with a large bulbous abdomen, probably a funnel-web, but this is a guess, because, as you know, Reg's body has never been found. In any case, the venom was powerful enough to kill him quickly.

We all stepped back several paces, leaving Reg and the spider (which was now frozen next to Reg's body) in the middle. 'All of you, come to this side,' said Jason.

Cautious, transfixed, Alastair and Nick moved round in a very wide circle as the spider darted over Reg's legs as if proud of its work. It was coming towards us until Nick, unprompted, threw a small stone which bounced into the grass a few inches from it – and it disappeared into the long grass and trees, away from us.

We were all frozen to the spot. 'Be careful, there may be more than one,' said Jason. But gradually Jason, Matt and I tiptoed forward and tried to help Reg. He wasn't yet dead, but had been bitten several times, including on his neck. We had no idea what to do and panicked, helplessly looking at each other, trying to think of a way to undo the damage – I'm not sure for how long; it felt like minutes, but could have been longer. Eventually, I laid Reg on his side and put him in a basic recovery position. I don't know what my logic was. I even shouted for help. Stupid.

Gradually, life left Reg: one minute there seemed some tiny hope, the next his eyes were open and blank. His breathing had stopped. I had never touched a dead body before, and never seen one for real before earlier that morning. My hands were shaking.

Reg was rolled on to his back, mouth open. Second spider or not, I began to cry, partly out of horror at the situation, partly for Reg, but also for myself. I felt guilty. Why didn't I look after him better? I promised that I would stay with him. I'd been stupid, so totally stupid, for not protecting Reg.

'This is bloody murder,' said Matt, also in tears. 'Someone did this on purpose. Look!' His foot was nudging a jar that lay in the grass. He bent down and with finger and thumb picked up a lid with tiny air holes.

Toby's death was like being shoved down a pit, and this was like finding that there was an even deeper and blacker place beyond that one. I was angry that I couldn't turn back time: if only I could go back ten minutes, just a tiny little ten minutes. Or go back to before it all started.

I was also filled with a desperate need to get to the next

shelter as soon as possible and call for help. I wanted to get the bodies buried, but the longer we were out there, the more dangerous things were – the police could deal with everything later. It terrified me that Nick was standing right with us and could kill us all at any moment. I decided to keep close by him and smash him with all my strength if he tried anything. What I had heard on the radio had largely gone from my mind – I wasn't sure if it was of any importance at all and was beginning to doubt that I had heard it correctly.

'There must be someone stalking us,' said Alastair. Again, like helpless antelope awaiting a lion's attack, we stared at the surrounding land.

My mind went to the girls' group, out there, somewhere, in the distance. Were they also under attack?

Lee interrupted my thoughts. 'That's not the only explanation,' he said. 'Take a look at one another. You may be looking at a [word deleted] killer.'

Alastair was sweating furiously, his eyes darting around. 'Then maybe we should scatter?'

'And have some sicko killer pick us off one by one? Or get lost and eaten by crocodiles? We're hundreds of miles from help, you stupid prick. We need to stick together and get to the next shelter,' said Nick.

Jason was silent.

'That's right,' I said, glaring at Nick, prepared to thump him and hope that Jason and the others helped me out. 'We need to stick together and keep a close eye on one another.'

Nick didn't miss what I was thinking. 'If you think I did this then you're even more *shit stupid* than you look. But I tell ya, if anyone tries anything on me, I'll split their head open. And that includes you, *Georgey*.'

Lee said, 'George's right. We need to get moving to the shelter and then get outta here.'

There was some muttering.

Matt stood a little closer to me.

Jason then spoke and we all turned to face him. 'No one is going to wander off on their own and be faced with God knows what. If we move quickly, we can radio for help and it'll be here really quick. We should all stay together as much as possible. Safety in numbers.' He saw us nodding in approval. 'Come on, let's get our stuff.'

I went to Reg's rucksack, took his waterproof from the side pocket, then ran back with Matt – the only person I could *really* trust – and draped it over Reg. I felt desperate and pathetic as I knelt next to the body. 'I'm so sorry, Reg.

I'll be back soon.' For a moment, the desire for revenge stirred inside me.

Our gesture was cut short by a cry from Jason. 'Come on, let's go!' Then, a few seconds later, a bellow: 'Georgey and Matt, where are you?'

'Not making a break for freedom?' said Nick. 'Or picking up something from the victim?'

I gritted my teeth. It made me even more determined to stay by Nick's side and, if need be, hit first, then ask questions later.

'Guys,' said Jason. 'This is important.' He was searching for something in his bag. 'Have any of you seen my maps and compass?'

We all shrugged. Lee caught my eye as he frowned, apparently in deep thought.

'They were here,' he said. 'In this outside pocket. I'm certain.' He searched all the pockets, then poured the contents of the main section on to the ground in front of us all. There was a first-aid box and a waterproof wrapped in a pouch, and one or two other useful odds and ends, but nothing remotely like a map or compass. He even checked his trouser pockets, though the maps would have been obvious there. 'Everyone – check your rucksacks,' he ordered.

175

I checked mine thoroughly. It suddenly occurred to me that these items might have been planted on me, like the gun had been, so I had a tiny feeling of relief when there was nothing there, but this was replaced by worry when I realized that they were definitely missing. I wondered if we could find our way back to the first hut if we had to. Probably – but, once you were lost in this landscape, you would stay lost.

'I don't understand,' said Jason. 'Not that it matters. I can remember the way: it's that hill over there. Not far.' He turned to Nick and me. 'Nick, you lead the way with me and, Georgey, you bring up the rear.'

'That's about right,' said Nick.

The journey wasn't quite as straightforward as Jason thought. There were a lot of points when he stopped or turned back, or looped round before carrying on, muttering to himself. I realized that I was hopelessly confused and couldn't retrace my steps. One clearing looked very much like another, and even the hills behind us were a line of sameness that disappeared into mist. The movement of the sun didn't help, not that I had any idea how to navigate by it anyway, so north could have been anywhere in a 90-degree arc.

Alastair probably knew the trick about pointing your

watch at the sun, but I didn't like to ask while Jason led us with purpose. And we were completely relying on him, walking in hopeful silence, thinking that each step brought us closer to escape.

We stopped just once, briefly, when there was about an hour to go. 'No one should leave my sight,' said Jason. 'Even if you want to piss.' He tried to make contact using the walkie-talkies – 'This is Ultimate Bushcraft calling for assistance' – though that was a vain hope and seemed less important now that we were near to Hut 2. I flicked through the channels, but there was nothing this time, even on channel 21, though I lingered there – making sure that no one saw me.

Soon we were off, traipsing up a slope with longer strides.

'Yes!' said Alastair as we saw the hut. 'Thank you, Jason. Thank God.'

Jason, Nick and Alastair ran ahead and entered within seconds of one another. It was smaller than the previous one, and made entirely of wood. Lee put his hand on my chest as I moved to overtake and reach the hut. 'Not so fast, if I were you. In my opinion, this isn't over yet, Georgey-boy.' I let my rucksack fall on the grass next to the others.

Strange thoughts fill your head at such times. I was immediately fearful of a sniper and moved to get my back to the building, but I also thought that Lee might be about to try something.

Swearing was coming from inside. 'What the f—' and similar.

'Quick, c'mon,' I said, and ran in with Matt, but Lee stayed.

The wires to the radio hadn't been cut this time – it was far wilder than that. The radio had been smashed to bits, probably by being whacked repeatedly against the table in the middle of the room. Bits of plastic, screws and wires were scattered everywhere. It was miles beyond repair. I felt like I'd been punched in the stomach.

'How the hell?'

[Here ends the eleventh part of George's statement]

THE OTHER CHAPTER 11
(SAID IN THE HOUR BEFORE):
HIM

Come on, then? Who helped me?

I CAN'T HEAR YOU!

Time is running out. You know that, don't you? You know that you're going to **die** <u>like all the others</u>.

I remember that first GLORIOUS day in the wilderness. I realized that one thing leads to another.

I know that you're keen to understand. Admit it: you must be *intrigued*.

I CAN'T HEAR YOU!

Toby, come quickly, oh please come quickly. Peter's outside and has fallen. Can you help me please oh please, great Toby one?

Please come quickly. He must be hurt. He needs your stupid help.

Look, there he is. Can't you see him?

Right there.

Right THERE!

Weeeeeeeeeeeeeeeeeeeeeeeeeeeeeeeeeeeeeeeeeeeeeeeeeeeeeeeeeeeeeeeeeeeee.

*BYE-BYE **Australian** Pie.*

Flatten this bush. Make it look like a fight.

YOU WERE ALL SO **STUPID**.

Then we went to the next hut.

BIG MISTAKE.

MASSIVE MISTAKE.

HUMUNGOID.

The game had begun. GAME ON!

My revenge on YOU.

Be in no doubt. It was all about <u>YOU</u>.

If you hadn't been so sickeningly **perfect**, it wouldn't have produced an allergic reaction in me.

<u>YOU</u> ARE TO BLAME.

Reg was asking for it more than anyone. He was pathetic.

I loved Sammy Spider. He slept nicely in a jar in my rucksack. Sneaky Spidey.

I bet even you wouldn't have been that brave. Would you?

I HATE YOU SO MUCH FOR BEING SO UNLIKE ME AND YET I THINK I WANT TO BE LIKE YOU.

THAT HAS DRIVEN ME MAD AND IT'S ALL YOUR SICK FAULT, YOU BASTARD.

I don't want you to die just <u>yet</u>.

The map and compass? I thought a bit of confusion might come in handy, so I hid them in the most brilliant place – Reg's stinking rucksack. There you were, within inches of the thing – if it was a spider it would have bitten you!

I AM PERFECTION AND I BET YOU'RE JEALOUS.

IF YOU'RE JEALOUS YOU CAN LIVE.

<u>Please</u> admire me.

And then *my young apprentice . . .*

He was already in the next hut. Damn near smashed that radio to bits.

Can you guess?

It's so bloody <u>totally</u> obvious.

BUT I can do better than tell you.

I CAN SHOW YOU.

Why don't I call him in?

Don't look so surprised.

HE WILL COME RIGHT HERE!

I love walkie-talkies. That's why I couldn't bear us to be without them. Boys and toys, eh?

Right. Channel twenty-one. That's the one.

Can you hear me?

Come out, come out, wherever you are.

Come out, come out, wherever you are . . .

EVIDENCE #3
TRANSCRIPT OF CONVERSATION BETWEEN A MEMBER OF THE ULTIMATE BUSHCRAFT GROUP AND THE OFFICE IN CAIRNS

At the end of Day 1 of the hike, the group checked in by satellite phone as expected. The line was bad, and the voice was incorrectly assumed to be that of Toby Jones.

Voice: G'day. Toby Jones with the Ultimate Bushcraft group checking in from Hut 1. All is well out here.

Cairns: Thanks, Toby, is that you? It's a bad line but I gather that everyone is OK.

Voice: Yep. No probs. All well. Please tell Andrea I won't be calling – [indistinct] time to think.

Cairns: OK, Tobes. As you want.

Voice: But all fine. Over and out.

Cairns: Understood. Over and out.

Subsequent attempts to contact the group were unsuccessful. This was the last contact made. Miss Andrea Brown's separate attempts to contact the group were also unsuccessful.

We stared at the smashed radio. There was despair with no wailing or aggression, even from Nick. Fear's icy hand grabbed my insides and squeezed. Despite the oppressive heat, I felt cold.

We stood inside the hut, silent and bewildered. This was broken by a scream from Matt which gradually turned into words: 'This-is-a-nightmare-and-I-want-it-to-end.'

Lee was different. He was still outside, now laughing hysterically, head back, eyes shut, bellowing.

'Will you both shut up?' said Nick. 'You'll be heard for miles around.'

'You stupid *kid*,' said Lee, still chuckling, approaching the doorway. 'There's only one other person for miles around and he's going to kill us all.'

'No one's gonna kill me,' said Nick. He ground his fist into his left hand. 'If I have to fight, I reckon I can smash anyone. No hillbilly with bad teeth and a banjo is going to make me squeal.'

Alastair spoke barely above a whisper. 'I think we

should all get inside and close the door.'

'And the difference that would make *is* . . . ?' started Lee. And yet he closed the door.

Matt was breathing deeply through tight lips. He looked to me for reassurance, not to Jason. 'Mate, I'm just scared and confused.' He had no humour left.

(I had no idea what to do. If I was back there now, I'd *still* have no idea what to do. You can't imagine how horrific it was. I kept on seeing Reg's blank eyes – and that spider – and I thought of Toby – and Peter, annoying though he was, was just a kid.)

Jason drew himself up to his full height. I thought that if he and I could stick together, we could fight off anyone, unless our opponent had a gun – but there was no evidence of a weapon, so far . . .

'I don't want anyone to panic,' Jason started.

Nick snorted.

'I don't want anyone to panic, but I want you to know that another big problem here is lack of water.' Jason glared at a neatly stacked collection of empty water bottles. 'You need to go steady with what you have.'

There was a lot of angry swearing (I remember someone's spit landing on my cheek). Someone had poured the water away and calmly put the large plastic bottles back into a neat group. Devious *and* menacing. That little detail worried me almost as much as anything else. It was evidence that someone was playing a game.

'Look,' said Nick, 'this means we're being hunted by someone *outside* this group. We're all *normal.*'

'Possibly,' said Lee. 'Maybe Toby and Peter heard someone outside the first hut and were killed when they investigated. Maybe someone crept up on Reg.'

I pushed from my mind the message that had disappeared from the table. Perhaps that was an honest mistake. Nick *certainly* couldn't have gone ahead and smashed the radio. Perhaps Reg's 'He-did-it' didn't refer to anyone in the group. Perhaps . . . Perhaps . . . But what about Luke's illness and my dodgy harness? Were they just accidents?

I could easily imagine Nick tying Reg's hands together and forcing a spider down his T-shirt. In fact, I thought that fingerprints or something would link him to the crimes; I'd seen on TV that it only took a tiny fibre to catch a murderer. Yet there was something about Nick's open aggression that didn't suggest him as a two-faced murderer – and that's why I didn't make a pre-emptive strike.

'We're going to have to spend the night here,' said

185

Jason. 'We all need to get some sleep and there's no way we're going to risk the darkness. But we need to make sure someone is always awake to keep watch.'

'Maybe two people should always be awake?' Lee suggested. 'Just to be *doubly* sure.'

'I doubt many of us are going to sleep much, but I agree that two people should always stay awake,' I said. 'How about Nick and I do the first watch?'

He grunted.

Jason's leadership was better than I expected. (But how we missed Toby! He would have known exactly what to do. He would have saved Reg's life, surely.) 'OK, I'll stay up with Matt from two a.m. until five a.m., and then Lee and Alastair can see us through the rest of the night,' Jason said as he pressed his hands together and pushed them to his chin, an unfamiliar gesture for him. 'We can probably all sleep in here, rather than in tents. I'm sure none of you would be idiotic enough to wander outside the hut.'

Outside the hut had already become a remote and lethal place.

But it was a small hut with no toilet, so it was only a matter of time before someone *had* to venture outside.

'I need a piss,' said Matt, peering through one of the

basic plastic windows. 'And I'm not going to do it in a bottle.'

I offered to accompany him. 'It can't be that dangerous. We've been outside all day and nothing happened while we stuck together,' I said.

'Be careful, Matt,' said Nick. 'You don't want to get caught with your pants down and Georgey nearby.' He just never stopped niggling at me.

Outside, the land was lit by the glorious early evening sun. We went a little way from the hut and looked around first before making two yellow rivers that ran away from us across the rock-hard soil.

'This ordeal won't go on forever,' I said to Matt after we had finished. 'If we keep going, and Jason can remember the way, we'll be at the next camp tomorrow – and, if that's wrecked, we'll meet up with the girls the day after at the planned halfway stop.'

Suddenly, I got the feeling that we were being watched. Maybe I heard a rustle. Maybe I saw a tree twitch. I nudged Matt.

'Look casual,' I muttered, but it took all my willpower to stand there fearing a bullet or an arrow at any second. I put my hand in front of my mouth to shield what I was saying: 'Matt, go back inside and press the bleep button on channel twenty-one of the walkie-talkie. Just keep pressing it.'

He didn't ask any questions, though it must have seemed like a really random request.

I knelt down and strained to hear. Incredibly, in the distance was the thinnest of bleeps straining to reach me on the breeze, not that I could work out exactly where it was coming from.

Jason and the others then came out of the hut. Matt must have been seen using the walkie-talkie, or perhaps he said something. In any case, they were making noise at exactly the time I needed complete silence.

'Is someone out there?' yelled Jason. 'You bastard! Come out where we can see you!'

Something stirred in the thickest part of the woodland, a few hundred yards away. It could have been an animal, but judging by the speed and size of the rustling, it was human. For an instant, there was a silhouette of someone – darkly dressed, or in shadow, it was hard to tell.

'I think that's a person,' said Alastair, his hand to his mouth. 'Oh my God.'

Nick swore strongly. 'I say we get the [word deleted].' He started down the slope and turned for support. 'Let's do this while we're all together.'

Jason was soon with him and I followed, calling to the others, trying to keep us together. We advanced as one group down the slope, but as soon as we hit the trees and undergrowth we became scattered. I couldn't tell if we were gaining on the person or not: they could have fled in any direction. And maybe it wasn't even a person in the first place.

'We need to get back together,' I shouted. 'Guys, we've got to go back.' Silence. I couldn't see more than a few paces in any direction through the bushes.

I wandered around for maybe ten minutes, but it might have been twenty. Every ten or twenty seconds I stopped and listened. Eventually . . . A snap. A rustle. I instinctively froze and went tense.

Behind me. Somewhere behind me. I breathed quietly through my mouth.

Nick was coming towards me. He was sweating and dirty. 'I can see that you didn't find anyone either. No surprise there. I fell over a branch and nearly broke my arm, but I'll be OK.'

'We should have stayed together by the hut,' I said. 'This is insane. If you lot had listened, I would have kept us organized.' I realize that this sounded annoying and I should have kept my mouth shut.

'Shut the [word deleted] up!' shouted Nick. 'If we weren't stuck out here, I would have smashed your pretty face in a long time ago.'

'Killing your thing, is it?' Again, it was a stupid thing to say.

'I just wanna teach you a lesson, Georgey. Make you show some *respect*. I don't wanna shank you, just grind your girly face into the dirt,' Nick snarled, and leant forward. We stared at one another for seconds that felt like minutes.

'C'mon,' I said, but without taking my eyes off him. 'We feel the same way, but we'd be stupid to take it out on one another here.'

Nick stared at me just as unwaveringly. 'Some other time . . .'

I walked off in the general direction of the hut, glancing over my shoulder a few times, just in case, but Nick kept his distance.

Suddenly I could see movement ahead – definitely a person this time – and turned round to beckon Nick on, hissing at him to catch up, our animosity instantly forgotten. *My enemy's enemy is my friend* is an expression I've heard since. Approaching slowly, unable to see clearly *and* stay hidden, I snapped a fallen branch and the figure turned around. I could just make out that it was Matt.

'God, George,' he said as I approached. 'Why are you creeping up on me? You nearly frightened me to death. This is hell.' He saw Nick just behind me. 'Hi, Nick,' he added, awkwardly.

'I know. We need to be more organized,' I said. 'But without Toby . . .'

'*You* need to organize us, George,' Matt said. (I wish I could have, but, despite what I'd said to Nick before, I didn't actually know what to do, the others wouldn't have followed me, and Jason was in charge – we were sixteen and he was twenty-one and those five years seemed to make a massive difference.)

Nick swore again and pushed past Matt, making him stumble backwards. With Nick disappearing into the distance, Matt came forward conspiratorially: 'Mate, I need to tell you something.'

'What?' I put my hand on his shoulder, but kept looking around warily.

'When we ran off, I kept the walkie-talkie with me. I didn't actually, you know, think to use it – my head is such a mess.' He whispered so that I could hardly hear. 'But then someone's voice was on it. Channel twenty-one. The one you mentioned before.'

'And what did it say?'

'Another one has bitten the dust. You know, like the song.'

'What?' I clenched my teeth and felt giddy. 'Had you heard the voice before?'

'No. Yeah. Probably not. Oh hell, I just don't know anything any more, George.' He strained to think. 'It wasn't a ranger, but there was something about it . . .'

I felt hysteria rise within me. We both knew what those words meant. *Another one has bitten the dust.*

'But, George, it's even worse. There was another voice. I'm sure it was a different one. It said *Good*. Really long and low: *Gooooooooooood*. And that was it.' Matt put his elbows into his chest and both hands to his mouth.

'We have to get back to the hut right now.'

We had some difficulty finding the hut even though it was on a hill that overlooked where we had been. Everywhere looked the same. Nick was there when we arrived, as was Lee – he said that he came back to the hut after ten or fifteen minutes as he knew from the start that running off was a stupid idea. 'Someone had to stay here and guard the bags. Someone brave and manly. But don't leave me alone again.'

I was beginning to be seriously worried. 'Have you

seen Al and Jason?' I asked.

He hadn't – Lee said that he hadn't heard or spoken to anyone at all.

As the four of us watched together, our attention was drawn to someone approaching. At first we could just see moving bushes and shadowy glimpses, but before long there was a distinct shape, and then Jason's ginger hair and grey T-shirt appeared. He was drenched in sweat and wiped his forehead. 'I went as far as an old dried-up stream,' he said, 'but I couldn't catch him, if anyone was ever there. I didn't see a thing. Where did you all go?'

'It was bloody chaos,' I said. 'We were all over the place. We *really* have to work together – like we said.'

Nick shot back immediately. 'And we *really* have to catch this bastard – before he catches us.'

'Or he catches Al!' I retorted. I let out a frustrated groan. 'I don't believe this. *Please* say one of you saw Al . . .'

No one answered. We all just stared at the trees. Fear rose and hope left with every passing minute. Matt and I shot one another anxious glances, but neither of us mentioned what he had heard on the walkie-talkie.

Another one has bitten the dust. It sounded sick. Like kids playing a game.

The sun fell below the western hills and darkness

descended fast. My mind was spinning about what to do. I couldn't very well go off on my own – if there were one (or two?) people out there I would be in big trouble if they jumped me in the dark. I didn't want to go with Nick, but neither did I really want to leave Nick with Matt, who I felt a special responsibility for (I know that sounds a bit excessive, but I did especially want to look after Matt). 'Matt, why don't we go and look for Al?' I said. At least that left Jason to keep an eye on Nick.

'Yes, OK,' said Matt.

Jason wasn't convinced that we should go off alone, but desperation was rising in me – it was nearly dark, and there's no way that Alastair would have stayed away from the camp unless something had gone wrong. 'OK, but keep in touch by walkie-talkie,' Jason insisted. 'And we'll keep our torches shining up here – though I wish you'd show me the respect I deserve and stay put.'

'Too right. Arrogant turd.' It was Nick, of course.

We took torches: they cast a pathetic light over distance though were very good up to about ten feet, so Matt looked left and me right as we walked together through the undergrowth. Some of it was impassable and we had to go round, but there were also a few clearings. But there was no sign of Alastair.

I was on channel 9. 'This is George. We haven't seen anything yet. Is Al back?'

Jason answered: 'Nothing yet.'

Then it was Nick, on another radio set: 'Don't be out there too long, you idiot. We're exposed up here and it'll be totally your fault if we're hacked to death by some lunatic.'

Finally, we heard Lee. 'We can see your torches. Don't drift too far left. You're going away from the course we took earlier.'

'Got it,' I said.

Soon after we left I got Matt to put his radio on channel 21. It wasn't too long after Lee's words that five clear bleeps came over that channel. Matt and I froze. A few seconds later there were three more.

'What the hell?' rasped Matt.

There were then more bleeps. We were transfixed, counting them, though we had no idea what it meant or who had sent it – or to whom.

Nine bleeps.

'Nine o'clock?' I mouthed, guessing. 'Or go to channel nine?'

We switched to channel 9, and a few seconds later a message came through: 'How much longer are you going to be out there?' It was Lee.

'Any sign of Al?' Now it was Jason.

Channel 21 was silent.

'George, is someone back there involved in this?' asked Matt. 'Do you think it's Nick?'

'I don't know,' I replied. 'But it's possible, yes. We need to watch one another's backs. I hate to say it, but I don't fully trust any of those three.'

We went round and round, contacting the others every now and again, perhaps revisiting places that we had already checked, perhaps finding new ones. It was impossible to tell. Hopeless – and no sign of Alastair. Our torch beams were yellow and flickering when we returned nearly an hour later.

The other three were still outside the hut when we returned. They had collected their rucksacks from where we'd all left them outside the hut and were sitting on them.

'We found nothing,' I said, dejected. 'Nothing at all. Let's get some sleep – we need to get going first thing tomorrow.'

'Like I said: arrogant turd. He thinks he's in charge. Jason's in charge.'

I ignored Nick and strode on, picking up my rucksack from where it was on the grass and going straight into the hut. But I immediately sprang back: lying on the table in the middle, his neck twisted round, ugly and terrible, tongue lolling out and eyes pointing upwards, was Alastair.

'Help! Help!' I shouted. 'Come here – all of you come here *right now*!' I screamed fully and loudly. There was absolutely no doubt that Alastair was dead.

Jason was the first to arrive. He pushed me back slightly and approached Alastair, looking carefully at his face. Then he retreated and all five of us stood in the doorway, reluctant to go in. Horrified.

'Try for a pulse,' said Matt from behind me. 'Maybe he's not dead. Maybe we can do something. Maybe this isn't as bad as it looks. Please. *Please*.'

'Matt – believe me, he's dead. Another one of us is dead.' I had seen people on television try for pulses in neck and arm, but had no real idea about what to do, so I crept forward and put my hand on his head by his ear and used my thumb to pull up his eyelid slightly. Alastair's head moved in a terrible way that I can't bring myself to write about. His neck had been broken with some force.

Matt was hysterical, screaming in short gasps and pleading for it all to end. I felt helpless.

Nick responded with a burst of aggression. 'We've

got to fight back. This is kill or be killed. We've gotta do something.'

Jason and Lee were silent. Was silence a strange response? Having been in the same place, full of the extreme horror of seeing such a thing, I'm not surprised. There is a place *beyond* panic where there are too many emotions. This time, I didn't cry.

I couldn't turn my back on Alastair's body so spoke to the others at an angle. 'Has no one been in here? I can't *believe* we didn't check in here! This is hell. Four people have died in twenty-four hours! We need to get help – now!'

We shuffled outside, switching on torches, shutting the door on Alastair.

'I want to get away from here,' said Matt. 'How did this all happen?'

I shook my head with confusion. Again, it just didn't make sense – the hut could only have been unattended for ten or fifteen minutes, if what Lee said was true. Unless Lee was responsible – but would he have had the strength to do that to Alastair?

'Our first rule is that no one goes into that cabin from now on,' I said. 'There's probably evidence in there that we need to leave for the police.'

Matt burst out with a torrent of words: 'I think we should all go separate ways – it's not safe together – and I think someone here has been involved in this – one of *you* is a sick killer or gone in the head and helping someone who is a sick killer.' He had lost control and wasn't thinking about what he was saying.

I grabbed hold of him. 'Matt,' I hissed to him through my teeth. 'You need to calm down, man. You've gotta be strong.'

'I know you're OK, George,' he said tearfully, clinging hold of my upper arm so tightly that it hurt. 'I just want this to end.'

Nick was furious. 'If that's the way you two benders feel, we're best off without you. Take your chances out there. Go on.' At least, that was more or less what he said.

'We're all scared and confused,' I said, standing my ground, refusing to let Nick's intimidation move me. 'And there's a *chance* someone here is involved.' I looked to Jason for support. 'But it's stupid to wander around out there in hundreds of miles of wilderness without a map.'

'No one has died while we've been together,' said Lee. 'And now there are only five of us. We need to stay together as a group at all times. With no exceptions. But there's no telling if the next cabin will be operational.'

Jason took his time. 'Agreed. We need to stay together. We will *have* to stay around here tonight, but can move on and find help tomorrow.'

'In two days we meet up with the girls,' said Nick.

'In two days we'll all be DEAD!' shouted Matt.

[Here ends the twelfth part of George's statement]

THE OTHER CHAPTER 12
(SAID IN THE HOUR BEFORE):
HIM

Another one has bitten the dust.

YEAH!

D'ya know? My helper was nearly caught when we arrived at the next hut.

We were using channel twenty-one, just as NOW.

He ran like a headless chicken – damn near broke his neck.

My MASTER PLAN was pretty well polished by then, but Alastair was a bonus. A bonus ball.

I was back there with him within two minutes.

This is silly. We'll be much safer at the hut, he said.

Safe? Bollocks. Absolute bollocks.

Shame, really. I quite liked Alastair. Interesting. He could have been a <u>pupil</u> if it had all turned out differently.

But I couldn't be there next to the body when everyone arrived back, could I?

COULD I?

I'll tell you the thing I really liked about my actual assistant. He <u>never</u> said no.

We started small. Incy-wincy small, on the first day,

with the fat one's clothes.

On the second day we started messing with Lukey's mind. He was scared and twisted <u>long</u> before we got to him. I began to realize my assistant and I might be able to do something SPECIAL together.

[Radio: I'm nearly there. Is he with you?]

Oh yes. He is very much here and very much ready for us to play with. Don't be long. He hasn't worked out who you are yet!

[Radio: laughter]

I couldn't have done it without my assistant.

I'll tell you another thing – but, hush, hush, it's a secret. You must promise not to tell.

He's doing it because he's a workman who enjoys his job. HA!

It's like pulling the wings off flies. Just better.

But it was always going to end up just the two of us, Georgey.

The final scene.

Greater love hath no man than he who lays down his friend for his life.

So you may want to look away when he arrives.

Because

it'll be

BYE-BYE.

And then we'll be alone at last and I CAN DESTROY YOU AND BE KING.

I remember standing with everyone by that hut after the radio had been smashed. AND I REALIZED THAT I WAS IN TOTAL CONTROL.

I

WAS

IN

TOTAL

CONTROL,

YET

IN

ANOTHER

WAY

I

CAN'T

CONTROL

MYSELF.

[Radio noise]

Ah. And here he is.

[Person enters]

TA DAH. Surprised?

NOTES FROM THE UNSOLVED CASE
OF GEORGE MURMAN, 1946

IN DECEMBER 1945, A BRUTALLY MURDERED WOMAN WAS DISCOVERED IN HER APARTMENT IN CHICAGO. THE MURDERER HAD WRITTEN A MESSAGE IN LIPSTICK ON THE WALL: *FOR HEAVEN'S SAKE, CATCH ME BEFORE I KILL MORE. I CANNOT CONTROL MYSELF.*

SIX MONTHS LATER, SEVENTEEN-YEAR-OLD WILLIAM HEIRENS WAS ARRESTED DURING A BURGLARY AND THE POLICE SAID HIS FINGERPRINTS MATCHED THOSE FOUND AT A MURDER SCENE.

WILLIAM HEIRENS WAS GIVEN A TRUTH SERUM AND INTERROGATED. UNDER THE INFLUENCE OF THE DRUG, HEIRENS SPOKE OF AN ALTER-EGO CALLED GEORGE. ACCORDING TO THE POLICE, DURING LATER QUESTIONING HEIRENS SAID THAT SOMEONE CALLED GEORGE MURMAN HAD COMMITTED THE MURDER OF THE WOMAN, AS WELL AS A NUMBER OF OTHER RECENTLY COMMITTED MURDERS. WHAT HEIRENS SAID WAS RECORDED, BUT THE TRANSCRIPT IS NOW MISSING.

HEIRENS DENIED THAT HE WAS GEORGE MURMAN.

He claimed he was innocent. Some say that the physical evidence is inconclusive.

We will never know.

Heirens died in prison in 2012, aged eighty-three.

CHAPTER 13
(18 HOURS BEFORE):
THE THIRTEENTH PART OF
GEORGE'S STATEMENT

The midnight darkness was absolute. This wasn't the darkness of the city, with a dull yellow glow in the sky and the sound of traffic in the distance. It was a sort of darkness that you don't get anywhere in England. It was as dark with your eyes open as with them closed.

That night was unlike any I've ever known. There were tents stored in the hut, which was too small to sleep in even if Alastair hadn't been in there. Jason and I went in to get them.

We put the tents up in silence. They were designed for two, but Jason, Nick and Lee all shared one. Despite the terror, as we lay down with Alastair dead just thirty yards away, I turned to Matt and said, 'Come on, Matt, mate. It's your job to say something funny.' It was partly to help Matt get back to normal; partly for myself.

Matt leant over to me and whispered, 'I wonder if they still make Batman underpants?' It was the silliest thing I've ever heard in my life. Sitting here now in a cell, typing this, I don't think anyone has said anything to me since that is remotely as funny. 'I wonder if they still make Batman underpants?' I'm not even sure *why* it's funny. But it was Matt's way of showing that he wanted me to know he wasn't going mad. I loved him for that.

It was horrible, getting tiny snatches of sleep and then being woken up by the slightest noise, sitting bolt upright, sometimes looking outside, but then realizing it was just a gust of wind or rustle of nearby leaves.

On one occasion I saw Jason looking out of his tent as I peered out of mine. We both clambered out and met halfway. He was holding the mallet that we had used to drive the tent pegs in.

'G'day, mate,' he said.

'Hi, Jase,' I whispered, a wary eye on the hammer. 'Have you seen anything?'

'No, mate,' he replied quietly. 'But I can't sleep. Feel . . . as if I'm needed.' This was a side to him I hadn't seen. He moved the hammer slightly. 'Just in case.' He squinted into the pitch black.

'I'll help you all I can,' I said.

'I know. Georgey, I'd really like you to see the real me.'

'Likewise,' I said.

'I promise you that I will be with you at the very end of all this.' He gave me a gentle mock punch and waited until I was back in my tent before he went back to his.

The wilderness came alive as soon as there was half-light, and after that I lay still, tired but a long way from sleep, and thought about the coming day – though the horrors of the past twenty-four hours kept tormenting me. We then heard Jason and Lee talking outside their tent and clambered out of our own to join them.

Jason reminded us that this was the most challenging of all the days: we had to pass along a narrow path – called, by Jason at least, the Devil's Crack – that led us to some kayaks and down a gentle part of the river. (The kayaks, we had been told before, were brought back as the group after us did the route in reverse.) 'I don't know any other way,' he said.

'Maybe we shouldn't wait two days to meet up with the girls,' said Lee. He was looking up and to the left as if trying to recall something he had seen. 'Can't we go downriver until it meets the sea? No one could track us down a river. Then we can go along the coast until we see someone?'

Jason thought it was a good idea to take our chances with the river.

Why didn't I run? Of course, I wish that I had. I wish I had taken Matt and run away with the other innocent pair. But the size of the place was beyond what you can imagine – it stretched endlessly, identically, in every direction. Even if we found water, how would we survive without food? We might walk round and round for days.

And, most importantly, at that time, I didn't know who to run *with*.

Nick was so unpleasant he had *killer* written all over him – but I wondered if he was too selfish to do something that would end up with him getting caught. Maybe he was just bad, not mad.

Jason had been nearly as unpleasant in his own way, though leadership had brought out the best in him. He had plenty of chances to lead us astray and had done all the right things. And he could have whacked me over the head with the mallet in the night and killed me there and then – no one would have known.

Lee? There was a deep weirdness about him. But I would have squashed him in a fight, and Toby certainly would. He might have been a nerdy mastermind, but a get-your-hands-dirty killer?

Matt? It didn't occur to me. Not in a million years.

I write this to show how confused I was. And I had to decide *right then*.

Before we left, I looked at Alastair again. He was still lying there, agony and shock frozen on his face. I wished that I had spent longer with him, got to know him better, included him in more things, made his last days fun. He was on the trip because he had been attacked, and now he was dead. I promised myself that if I ever got through this I wouldn't waste a single day ever again.

We walked for over two hours in the same order: Jason then Nick then Lee then Matt, with me last. As before, I liked being at the end, apart from the need to keep looking behind. We went down and down into the valley, then began to go up towards the cliff path. We pushed ourselves hard.

The midday sun burnt down on us, but we had to move as quickly as possible.

Jason was certain it was the right way. 'There it is,' he said. 'The Devil's Crack.' It was a narrow pass through a line of hills that looked like it had been chiselled out by a giant.

The path, which was little more than two paces wide, was about halfway up a steep and high slope – rocks hung down from above and there was a vertical drop below. I felt uneasy as I remembered Toby and Peter and what had happened to them. But it would have taken a lot longer to climb up the hillside and then get down the other side – and, more than anything, I just wanted this to be over.

Jason stopped. 'This is the one part of the whole journey that has been prepared. In about fifty-metre lengths, a rope is threaded through bolts hammered into the cliff. We're meant to go very slowly and attach ourselves with our ropes.' In the outer pocket of our rucksacks we all had a basic harness and rope.

'Forget that,' said Nick. 'We just hold on with our hands and get through as quickly as we can. Health and safety is the last thing we need to worry about.'

'You're right, mate,' said Jason. 'The path is wide enough, and we need to get to the river as soon as poss.' Jason then said he would go last in case anyone got into difficulties.

I agreed that the longer it took the more dangerous it was – and, again, I couldn't foresee what would happen next. Somehow, I ended up going first.

It was a spectacular setting and just for a split second my mind drifted to thinking that it would have been an awesome place to visit in different circumstances. (Normal thoughts did creep into your mind even with all of that horror and shock.) The path wasn't difficult to walk along, but it was knotted with roots – trees were dotted around, clinging to the side of the cliff, forcing their roots into the thinnest of cracks.

About halfway along, at the very worst point, rocks started falling from above. At first it was just a pebble or two, but then they were proper stones that would crack your head open if they landed on you. Either a mini-avalanche was happening, or someone was throwing or kicking them down. We all retreated right next to the cliff, hands on our heads as a feeble attempt to shield ourselves.

After a brief pause, I looked up to see a white stone the size of my hand heading straight towards me at terminal velocity. I flipped my head out of the way – the stone missed me by inches and bounced down and down, breaking up as it went and then shattering completely on the rocks below. The next stone thumped on to my rucksack and ricocheted out and downwards before exploding on a boulder at the bottom. But at this point I was shielded by an overhanging rock.

I could see the next two in the line, Lee (behind me) and Matt (coming round the corner), dodging stones in the same way. Sooner or later one of us was going to get hit.

'I'm turning back!' Matt said. But Lee kept on coming until he was alongside me, under the same overhang.

'You go first,' I said. 'Put your rucksack over your head and go for it.'

Lee then made a break for it, one stone hitting his hand as it held his rucksack, drawing blood immediately.

I decided to run for it as well, rucksack also held over my head. This would get me to where Lee was, on the path round the corner ahead where rocks didn't seem to be falling. But it was an uneven track, and I had to keep glancing up to see if more stones were on their way. It took a split second to catch my foot on a twisted tree root and go sprawling forward. It was terrifying – my legs buckled and I went flying through the air, unable to stop myself, and then slid forward pathetically towards the edge. My rucksack went ahead of me, and the momentum kept me going until – despite struggling for anything to hold on to, something to stop my trajectory – I went over the edge.

And then I stopped, dangling helplessly, holding on to a tree root that was slowly freeing itself from the rocks, sending rock dust down into my face.

I heard one thud, presumably my rucksack bouncing off the cliff below, and then another more distant one as it hit the bottom.

'Help!' I shouted. 'Somebody help!' I was dangling by one arm, struggling to get the other one up for a more secure hold. 'Help! Somebody help!'

But Lee had run ahead and Matt had stayed back.

I glanced down. The simple truth was that if I let go I would die. This wasn't the forty feet of a Climbers' Kingdom-type adventure park climb; this was a couple of hundred feet of freefall before smashing on to boulders below.

'Help! Help me!' I knew that I couldn't hold on forever, and that the root was getting weaker and weaker as it was dragged further out of the cliff face.

The rocks had stopped falling, though, and I heard a voice: Jason's. 'Georgey?' he said. 'Georgey?'

'I'm here! Please! Help!' My words came out in desperate snatches.

A face appeared above. Jason looked at me and then at the huge drop below. His eyes widened. 'You're going to have to trust me,' he said. 'You're going to have to put your life in my hands.'

We were completely alone. If he was the killer, this was his perfect opportunity. No one would ever know. I simply would have fallen off the cliff.

Like Toby and Peter.

'I trust you,' I said, looking into his eyes.

'That's what I want to hear,' he said, and he described how he was bracing himself by putting his foot into a crack in the path and holding a root with his right hand. Then his left hand came towards me.

It was a struggle for me to reach up, but I managed to hold his hand and help him pull me up by scrabbling with my feet and then . . .

I had to let go with my other hand.

For two or three seconds nothing held me up apart from Jason's grip – my life was in his hands. My feet dangled above the abyss below as I was heaved back up to the path.

Then I was able to hold on to a different root, one on the path itself, with my right hand. My legs swung up and I was safe – right on the edge, lying parallel to the drop, but out of immediate danger. Jason looked down at me again, and for a terrible moment I thought he was going to push me off – but then he hauled me back and helped me to my feet.

'Go forward to the end of the track,' he said. 'Nick and Matt are back there and I want to help them through to safety. I *wonder* whether the rockfall was man-made or natural.'

I went on very carefully, staying as far away from the outside of the ledge as possible, feeling pretty shaky. Lee was waiting for me at another overhanging section that was right next to the point where the rocky path turned back to thick vegetation on a gentle decline down to the river.

'Everything OK?' asked Lee. 'You took your time.'

'I slipped,' I said, my voice trembling. 'But Jason rescued me. He saved my life.'

Just imagine being able to say that about someone: HE SAVED MY LIFE. It does make you see someone differently.

[Here ends the thirteenth part of George's statement]

We arrived at about 16:45 this afternoon (Thursday 30 July). It was a standard call-out because of the failure of a parallel girls' team to make contact with the group. Initially, Constable Farrer and I found nothing out of the ordinary at the site.

As routine we then checked the static radio, which was found not to be working. Upon further investigation we ascertained that wires had been cut. But there was no sign of a disturbance and the group seemed to have left peacefully.

We contacted the station and undertook a routine scan of the surrounding area. The topography there is challenging, but we proceeded along the path that went round the outcrop of land surrounding the hut. During this investigation, we saw a body among boulders at the bottom of a cliff.

It appears that the fatality was caused by injuries sustained in a fall. The cause of that fall is still a matter of speculation, and evidence at the scene was inconclusive.

We again contacted headquarters and asked for helicopter assistance.

The whereabouts of the remaining members of the group are currently unknown.

There has been no formal identification yet of the fatality discovered at the scene, but we believe it to be Mr Toby Jones, the group leader.

Initial report filed by email at 19:14 on Thursday 30 July.

THE OTHER CHAPTER 13
(SAID IN THE HOUR BEFORE):
HIM

You can stop playing dead now, Peter.

Pretty clever, eh?

It's so easy to play dead. You just lie there! Fooled everyone. Toby – that snivelling piece of nothing – was dead, and once you've seen one dead body you've seen them all.

HA!

You did well, Pete. We really fooled them, didn't we?

I knew you'd find us. Couldn't miss the boats, and this hill does look like a tit. But *well done*.

Pete, look – we have someone to look after. Someone I SAVED for us.

Pete and I have something AMAZING in common. We both share an *interest*.

Pete here has had some terrible problems. He's been a <u>very</u> naughty boy. Not quite right in the head. Or that's the way they see it. So Mummy and Daddy sent him on a trip so that he could become so much better.

We had great fun with fat Reg's clothes and Lukey's

dreadful **out-of-all-proportion** fear of us re-enacting some of his past with him.

And then we really got into our stride, didn't we, Pete?

NOW, I want you both to listen.

YOU first.

And then you, Petey.

Why did you have to do everything as if you were so perfect, Georgey?

Right to the last. Even sitting there now, I can see those stupid tolerant eyes.

I'll come back to YOU.

Pete. Come here.

I couldn't have done it without you.

They shouldn't send naughty boys like you on these trips. It just gives you an <u>opportunity</u>.

You always did everything **perfectly**.

But I have to tell you something.

Peter Pan, you've played your part and now it's time to EXIT. It's time for you to fly with the other Lost Boys. I have to be here alone with him – that's the plan. It's our destiny.

Come this way and you can leave in a civilized manner.

No. Don't try to struggle.

DON'T YOU DARE TRY TO STRUGGLE!

You've done your work and

now YOU HAVE TO GO.

LET'S GO TO THE EDGE TOGETHER.

COME ON.

I'll go over with you if you like. Really, I will. If that's what it takes.

GOING GOING GOING GOING GOING GOING GOING GONE.

Thank you, Petey.

It was good while it lasted. But a worker has to realize when his job is done.

He's nothing compared to you, Georgey.

YOU'RE ONE MAIN CHARACTER. AND I AM THE OTHER. The rest are just *nothing*.

<u>And now we're all alone at last.</u>

HA!

Does that hurt?

Your powers are weak.

THE END IS NEAR.

221

CHAPTER 14
(SIX HOURS BEFORE):
THE FOURTEENTH PART OF
GEORGE'S STATEMENT

Lee and I leant against the cliff and stared at the river. It had been completely hidden by the hills we had just cut through, but now it dominated the huge valley, slowly finding its way through the flat landscape.

Voices appeared – three of them. For a lifetime, I had taken it for granted that people emerged from cliff paths alive, but after everything that had happened I wasn't sure of anything any more. I was relieved to see Matt in particular, but also Nick.

'There was some bastard up there!' spat Nick. 'That wasn't coincidence.'

Though I never saw a glimpse, I'm sure Nick was right, and there was someone up there, dislodging stones at the very top of the cliff – stones that then gathered others as they fell, stones that nearly killed me.

We were all confused and (apart from me) told little extracts of what had happened to us.

'I think we should move on,' I said. 'If someone is up there, we're not safe.'

First, though, we paused to take a drink from a fairly small waterfall that was coming out of the rock face. The water was surprisingly cold, massively refreshing, and we drank all we could. The others filled their bottles.

Jason came over and put his hand on my shoulder. 'I'm so pleased that you've come through this.'

To have been so close to death and survived: it changes you. I'm sitting in my cell writing this in the half-hour before we're ordered downstairs to eat. My room-mate is staring at me and telling me to make it good and introduce some naked ladies (or words to that effect). There's a metal door and a metal bed and it smells a bit of urine. But I'd rather be here than at the bottom of that narrow canyon, smashed to bits. If I ever get out of here, I'll try to do good for the rest of my life.

We went down the broad slope towards the river. The vegetation was much thinner, and going downhill we made really good time. But the riverbank wasn't a neat boundary between land and water. It was sometimes marshy, and that meant possibile crocodiles. We thought we saw some sliding into the river in the far distance while we were looking for the boats and it made us wary.

Without a compass or map we didn't arrive in exactly the right place for the kayaks, and we spent almost two hours looking for them – for much of the time searching in completely the wrong direction. Eventually we took the chance that they were upstream and had what I thought at the time was our one stoke of luck.

All five of the two-man kayaks were there. We seemed to be making actual progress. I dared to think that we might get out of it alive, and then leave the police to work out who was responsible.

Jason explained that the original plan of Ultimate Bushcraft was to go downstream for about ninety minutes – it was the gentlest part of the river – then walk to the next hut. He thought he could remember the way.

'I think we should just keep on going,' I said. 'It'll put distance between us and . . .' I didn't finish the sentence. 'We can travel so much faster with the flow of the water, and we're bound to find someone on a river or by the coast.' I didn't mention it, but I also couldn't bear the thought of going to another cabin.

Matt nodded. 'I'm with George.'

'I agree,' said Lee, pointing to the north. 'That way just takes us further into the middle of Cape York and away from any sort of human life. Rivers are arteries. They attract people.'

Nick shrugged. 'It's all luck. Blah-bloody-blah.'

Jason took a boat on his own, Nick went with Lee in one boat and I went with Matt. The logic was that Jason, Nick and I were the more powerful and could keep the same pace.

It was Jason's idea to hide the remaining two boats in case someone was following. We didn't take them far, but they were dragged up on to the bank and hidden under a bush. It would have been almost impossible for them to be found – unless the person following us was told where to look . . .

The first section of the river was easy to navigate and we made steady progress. Trees dipped down into the river on either side and sometimes cut into the channel, but it was easy to glide past them. My arms ached, and I could see that Nick and Jason were also straining. Each stroke, I said to myself, was one I wouldn't have to make again – one nearer freedom.

Jason, who was on his own in a kayak and slightly ahead, stopped just before a sweeping curve in the river and explained that it was at this point that Ultimate Bushcraft would usually cut across country to the third hut. This was our last chance to take that route. If we went on, it was also burning the chance to meet with the girls' group in thirty-six hours or so, to have the safety of far greater numbers, and access to working radios.

The river and the possibility of a quick rescue, or a couple of days, including one more night, of battling through the wilderness?

I will never know what the right decision was. But we went on, down the river. Rolling the dice.

After about ninety minutes we found that we no longer had to paddle. Another fairly big river had joined ours and that significantly increased the flow of water.

Good: more speed. Quicker escape. Faster rescue.

The hills on either side also hemmed the river in, forcing it left and then right, and then squeezing it downhill.

We were guided into the first set of rapids gradually. We saw the curls and splashes of water grow and had a chance to talk to one another and think about our descent. Jason went down first, then Nick and Lee, and then Matt and myself. We dipped and wobbled, but there was never any real danger of falling out until the end, when there was a steep ten-foot slope. We pointed our boats downwards and let the river take us. In other circumstances it would have been fun, but no one smiled or whooped. We knew that one mistake could cause a delay or cost a life – potentially both. It was agonizing.

Behind us, birds cartwheeled through the sky and the

forest hummed with life, but there was no other boat within sight.

We all tried our walkie-talkies from time to time, but, again, nothing.

'If you can hear us, we're heading down the river,' was said more than once into channel 9.

I believe that someone was also using their walkie-talkie as a way to communicate with the person who was coming after us.

Someone did hear. And someone did follow.

But in any case, even if I'd been certain we were being followed, it would have been stupid to keep radio silence when we were so desperate for rescue. The girls were only thirty miles or so away. Had we known their course better, we would have battled upstream and been saved. But we were ignorant.

The second set of rapids were upon us before we realized what was happening. The river, now threateningly hedged in by cliffs, went into a jagged 'S' bend and rocks jutted up beneath the surface.

'Can we stop?' shouted Lee, foam splashing in his face. 'This is dangerous.'

It was difficult to steer at all – there was no way that we could reach the side. Turning back, even slowing down, was impossible; we were like corks being swept down a drain.

There was no sign of it ending. Curve came after curve and large rocks sometimes blocked the way. We were nudged and shoved, the kayaks scraping against rocks that hid themselves just below the surface. The boats dipped down and up; angry water soaked us. It was beyond what we could cope with and beyond what the boats were designed for.

Jason's boat was carried ahead. Maybe this was because it was lighter, or perhaps he just happened to find a faster course. Matt and I were next, but then we were dashed forward, nearly tipping out, and careered into the bank – and were caught in one of the few pools that were there. I dug my paddle between two rocks and held it firm. Perhaps we would be able to clamber out and make our way along the rocks that ran alongside the channel?

Nick and Lee sped past us. Their faces were a mix of terror and gritty determination. Then they were gone, disappearing into the distance and then round the next bend in the river.

It was soon obvious that Matt and I wouldn't be able to get out of the kayak and that I wouldn't be able to hold it in position forever.

'Just keep us here as long as you can!' shouted Matt.

I knew that we'd have to brave it sooner or later, but we were recovering our composure and strength, and the few minutes that we paused made the final leg of the rapids easier – easier, but certainly not easy. I pushed us away from the rocks and we were soon to our limit again, all our power used to stay upright and inside the boat rather than actually steering.

Finally, we came to the most extreme set of rapids – more of a stepped waterfall.

A wide, calm lake surrounded by drooping trees was in the distance. Beyond it, the river, now very broad and lazy, continued to the sea.

A *calm* lake? Only in one sense.

One part of my brain was concentrating on getting down the cascading drop, but another part was taking snapshots of what was in the distance.

In the first frame I saw Nick swimming to one side, away from his upturned boat.

(All the time, I was concentrating on keeping our kayak level in the water.)

An instant later, I caught sight of Jason, further in the distance, mouth wide as he bellowed, an oar above his head in anger or anguish or both.

As we splashed down into the lake, for a split second I saw Lee to the right, in the water, being smothered by crocodiles. There were three, each perhaps ten feet long, slipping over one another, competing for the kill. (I've been told that they were probably saltwater crocodiles, about as far upstream as they ever venture. If so, they can kill cattle and horses – people are small fry.)

I'm sorry, but I can't bring myself to describe the scene properly.

Nick was swimming away towards the shore on the opposite side to Lee, his paddle still in his hand.

'Go back and help him! Go back and help him!' shouted Jason, who was now paddling towards Lee as fast as he could.

It was too late. The three large crocodiles had done their work: Lee was submerged and had stopped making any noise. A deep red cloud was rising up through the water.

I immediately angled our kayak towards Lee but the crocodiles were aggressive, fired by the taste of blood, and one swam towards us, bumping into the boat, snapping furiously, razor-like teeth thrashing around in the water. Roaring with frantic desperation, I beat down at the creature with my paddle, smashing its broad snout and then jabbing for its eye. On another day it could easily have bitten my arm and dragged me into the water. I've been told since that I was *very* lucky (and I know that some doubt this part of the story – but it is completely true). Then, perhaps because I *was* lucky, perhaps because it felt there was easier food to be had, it slid away; but it was too late, too late for Lee.

'What have you done?' shouted Jason. 'Why did you do that?' At first I thought he was shouting at me, that we had done something wrong, but then I saw Jason was focused solely on Nick.

Nick's kayak had filled with water and was bobbing around at the edge of the area that was tinged with blood. He had now dropped his paddle and was swimming powerfully towards the side.

Jason called over to me and we paddled our kayaks towards one another. Matt was shaking, gazing vacantly ahead, his knees pulled into his chest.

Jason hissed through clenched teeth: 'Did you see that? Did you see what he did? The bastard! They arrived, paddled around for a bit, and Nick saw the crocodiles and tipped the boat over. Lee was helpless – he just splashed around in the water, crying out in terror, until the crocs grabbed him.' He glanced in Nick's direction, seeing him reach the shore. 'I always thought that it was Nick.'

Confidently, ferociously, Jason looked me in the eye. 'We have to do something about this. We have to stop Nick before he kills the rest of us.'

What follows is probably the hardest part of the account for me. You have to understand that Jason had just saved my life, and that we had seen Lee killed, and that Nick had been malicious throughout the entire trip. Jason was also the closest we had to an adult. Who would not have tried to control Nick – to deal with him before we were killed like the others?

Matt spoke quietly. 'He's going to kill us. I don't want to die.' Even quieter: 'I don't want to die. My life has hardly started.'

I'm not blaming Matt one bit, but I agreed. If we didn't do something, Nick was *surely* going to murder us all. With Jason, I could do something – but on my own? And if Nick was somehow left with Matt, there would be no contest.

'Come on, Georgey,' said Jason. 'We can do this if we work together. If you don't help me, *you'll* be responsible for our deaths.'

I saw a need to do something dangerous, possibly bad, to save us from something much worse. 'We'll have to tie him up and force him down the river with us in a boat.'

Jason nodded. 'We can pin him down and tie his

hands with one of the safety ropes.'

Nick had now reached the other side, dragged himself out of the river and was warily standing about three or four feet off the ground on a tree branch that was bent at a 45-degree angle over the water. The crocodiles had slipped out of the river on the opposite bank.

We drifted closer, silent about our intent.

Nick swore several times. 'I – I – can't believe that happened.'

We reached the edge of the pool and our kayaks grounded on rocks. Still without a word, Jason and I climbed out of our boats, splashed through the water, and strode towards Nick. I felt nervous; I'd never been in a proper fight before. Matt stayed in the boat, paralysed into silence and confusion by what had happened to Lee.

Nick was the most timid I had ever seen him, but I thought that was because he had been caught committing a terrible murder. Perhaps even he had limits? Perhaps he knew that we were coming for him?

Did I wonder whether helping Jason was right? No, I didn't sit down and write a list of arguments for and against. You can't understand if you haven't been in that sort of position. It just seemed *obvious*. I thought I was going to die.

It's not easy to write this, you know.

Jason had a cold determination. 'Why did you do that?' he asked. 'I saw it all. You [word deleted] murderer.'

To begin with, Nick was startled. Then he stubbornly protested for a bit in a way that wasn't like the usual Nick. 'How can you say that, man?' he said to Jason. 'You saw it.'

I was sure that Nick was manipulating us.

'LIAR!' Jason's hands were fists.

I remember that after the word *liar* Nick snarled in his usual way: 'What the hell are you talking about? The kayak just tipped as we fell down that thing.' He pointed to the waterfall in the distance. 'There was nothing I could do.' He stared at us. 'You two can go to hell.'

'This has got to end,' I said. 'You can't do it again, Nick.'

'Do *what* again?' replied Nick. 'And what do *you* think you're going to do? Eh?' He was now preparing to fight, standing upright, jutting his chest out.

'Now!' Jason shouted, and we both surged forward.

Nick was quick to react. He threw a punch at Jason – connecting with his cheek – and kicked me in the upper leg.

We were immediately upon him again, throwing punches ourselves, but Nick was sturdy and aggressive. Within seconds we were grappling with him rather than throwing punches – it was chaos, a tangle of legs and arms – and then all three of us collapsed to the ground, jarring ourselves on rocks, still punching and scratching and holding and stamping. I discovered that real fights are not easy to remember; they are punch and counter-punch, all happening at the same time, squirming and shoving and swearing.

If only Nick had stopped – but he would never give up. Even when we had him pinned down, we couldn't turn him over to tie his hands; he continued biting and jostling, using his knees and elbows and fists. After a brief lull, he was at us again – and his fist caught me straight in the nose. A red-hot bar of excruciating pain was slammed through my face. I retaliated in exactly the same way, partly out of anger, partly out of fear.

But even this didn't quell Nick's desire to fight; if anything, it was inflamed. Nick's fist made contact with Jason's lip and there was an explosion of blood.

Jason was forced back for an instant, then retaliated by striking Nick hard on his left cheek, then nose, then forehead and eye. While Nick was dazed, I managed to get both my hands round his neck and hold his head to the ground, pinning him down by kneeling either side of his chest.

We *could* have stopped then. We *should* have stopped then. We had the rope, and Nick was beginning to fight less. But Jason suddenly brought a stone crashing down on the side of Nick's head. Nick was knocked out and stopped struggling.

Jason brought the stone down again.

Nick was still. He didn't breathe. As I understand it, he died at that moment.

I think it was two or three seconds before I let go. Blood had dribbled from Nick's mouth and was heading towards my hands. I was mesmerized, adrenalin pumping, knees still either side of Nick's chest, while the trail of blood ran down and dripped from the side of Nick's cheek on to the stone that Jason had used. Jason, not me.

Matt's voice jarred me back to the present. He was still in the kayak: 'Is he dead?'

Nick's hand was on my leg, but it flopped away on to the ground.

'Yes,' I answered. 'He's dead.'

'It's all over,' Jason said. 'I can look after you on my own now. It's finished.'

'Yes,' I said, not really thinking of anything. 'But I wish it'd finished differently.' I never actually wanted Nick dead, even if he had shown absolutely no mercy to others.

I didn't want Jason to do what he did with that rock. But he couldn't have done it without me.

We drifted away from the body and sat away from the river on rocks. Matt, zombie-like, came to join us. I squeezed his shoulder a bit, to reassure him.

'He deserved to die,' said Jason. 'He was *nothing.*'

'No one deserves to die,' I said. 'Everyone should be given the chance to become good, even if some people never get there.'

'That's the sort of thing I'd expect from someone like *you*,' said Jason. 'I used to think that you were *pretending* to be perfect, but now I wonder if you are *perfect* in your own narrow, unimaginative, sickening way.'

I thought this was a completely crazy thing to say (I look at those words now on the screen and they seem even madder) – I told him that I just wanted to be myself, that things just emerged in the way they did without me trying to be one thing or another.

'George,' Matt asked. 'What are we going to do now?'

'I'm in charge, remember,' said Jason, his voice rising. 'You must remember that.'

[Here ends the fourteenth part of George's statement]

THE OTHER CHAPTER 14
(SAID IN THE HOUR BEFORE):
HIM

WAKE UP, WAKE UP.

GEORGEY, WAKE UP. GEORGEY FLEET.

GEORGEY FLEET.

GEORGE FLEET.

I AM STILL TALKING TO YOU.

I HAVE BEEN TALKING TO YOU, AND YOU'VE HARDLY BEEN LISTENING.

LISTEN TO UNCLE JASON.

Listen to me, Georgey.

Let me sit next to you.

The best bit of all was when I told you Nick was guilty. I had control over you at last. I was pulling your strings – you were my puppet. I was the puppet master.

I AM TRULY THE KING OF THE WORLD.

When this is over, I will be the new George. YOU will be finished. De-Georged.

Then the Matts will think of *me*; and the Tobys will follow *me* and talk of *me*.

How many lives have you saved? Not as many as

I have finished.

I win.

How I hate you.

BUT I WANT WHAT YOU HAVE.

You're just a stinking thief, people like you, stealing from people like me.

Your fancy family and cosy house and girlfriend – girlfriend<u>s</u> wanting you to do things to them.

WHY NOT ME?

WHY NOT ME?

WHY NOT ME?

<u>But from now on it *will* be me.</u>

SAY SORRY BEFORE IT IS ALL OVER.

SORRY FOR THE THINGS YOU ARE GUILTY OF.

Come on.

STAND UP ON YOUR FEET AND SAY SORRY.

A REMINDER OF A
MISCARRIAGE OF JUSTICE

A TRUE STORY:

TIMOTHY EVANS'S WIFE AND YOUNG DAUGHTER WERE KILLED IN 1949. EVANS HIMSELF WAS CONVICTED OF THE MURDER OF HIS DAUGHTER AND KILLED BY HANGING IN 1950.

AN OFFICIAL INQUIRY CONDUCTED FIFTEEN YEARS LATER CONCLUDED THAT THE TRUE KILLER OF EVANS'S DAUGHTER HAD BEEN A MAN WHO LIVED IN THE SAME HOUSE AS EVANS, SOMEONE CALLED JOHN CHRISTIE. CHRISTIE WAS ALSO RESPONSIBLE FOR THE DEATH OF EVANS'S WIFE, AS WELL AS HIS OWN WIFE AND SIX OTHER WOMEN.

THE POLICE MADE SERIOUS MISTAKES WHEN SEARCHING THE HOUSE AT RILLINGTON PLACE, MISSING REMAINS OF EARLIER VICTIMS IN THE GARDEN AT THE BACK OF THE PROPERTY. THEY ALSO FORGED CONFESSIONS FROM EVANS.

CHRISTIE WAS THE CHIEF WITNESS *AGAINST* EVANS AT HIS TRIAL BECAUSE THE POLICE BELIEVED ALL HIS STATEMENTS.

THIS FALSE TESTIMONY WAS VITAL IN BRINGING A GUILTY DECISION AGAINST THE INNOCENT TIMOTHY EVANS.

After the death of Nick, we were again faced with tough choices about what to do.

Matt was slowly beginning to calm down and communicate, and all three of us agreed that it would be best to continue towards the sea in the boats, but Jason repeatedly stressed that this was completely his decision, not ours. 'I'm in charge of things. Not you. I'm the leader,' he said. As we went down the river, I wondered whether I had made a terrible mistake. Jason was very agitated and aggressive – almost as if he was drunk or on drugs.

For a time, the land around us was flatter, but craggy land gradually appeared again and Jason suggested that we rested. 'If the great Georgey thinks it's acceptable, we'll stop,' Jason said. He always referred to me as Georgey – never George, not even as 'you'. I hadn't noticed it before.

What happened next was terrible. A few seconds after I had stepped out of the boat there was a searing pain

241

to the back and side of my head. I fell to the ground – blotches appeared in front of my eyes and grew into dizziness every time I tried to raise my head. I tried to ask a question, but it came out in a muddled, muttered mess, as if the cords that operated my mouth had been cut. Out of the fog came an understanding that my hands were being tied. I was then kicked three or four times in the side; there was excruciating pain and I felt, and heard, a rib crack.

Still dazed, I could see Matt being thumped repeatedly. Over and over and over again. Twenty or thirty times. Imagine that. I can't tell you what it was like, watching, unable to do anything. I was just able to get my head off the ground a few inches and croak, 'Stop!'

Jason paused. 'This is *punishment*,' he said. 'He should NEVER have followed YOU in that way. He *should* have followed ME.' Jason chuckled. 'Watching this is **punishment** for YOU.'

Pure evil. Just scratch the surface and there it was lurking below. I've been asked about this by one of the psychiatrists helping my lawyer. I don't know if Jason was confused in some complicated psychological way – all I knew at the time was that he was just a very manipulative, malicious person, masked as someone reliable and trustworthy. You just can't tell, can you?

Jason tied Matt's hands behind his limp body and shoved him face-down into a kayak. Jason pushed the kayak out into the river and the current took it.

'You can't say that isn't fair. He stands a chance. I'm too generous. I'm the KING,' Jason said to me with a smile.

But Matt was probably already dead. As you all know, the kayak was found upturned in the river, his body nowhere to be seen. I don't believe he suffered after the first two or three knocks to the head.

Of all of them, it's Matt's death that makes me wildest with anger. Matt had become one of my best friends in a very short time. Now I was alone.

I knew that I was dealing with someone totally deranged and beyond reason. If only I had Nick with me.

I had been so stupid.

I pleaded with Jason, trying to reason with him, begging him to stop. 'Jason, please listen to me,' I said. 'This can all end OK.' I was being marched up a hill and then, after that, up a steep slope. 'Please listen to me.'

'Shut up! Now it's MY turn to speak. If you know what's good for you, you'll listen. Just you and me. At THE END of the story. You know that this is not a happy ending. No. Not happy FOR YOU at all. But you <u>deserve</u> an <u>un</u>happy ending. And they all lived <u>un</u>happily ever after. Because that's what they **<u>DESERVED</u>**.'

Jason said crazy things. He told me about a boy he had killed by pushing him in front of traffic and another he killed in a quarry. I remember him telling me about getting caught stealing a chicken, and then getting the job with Ultimate Bushcraft, but lying about his past. I know that all these things are being investigated right now. I certainly haven't made them up.

I winced with pain as Jason punched my side, hitting my broken rib.

'You can laugh. You can laugh right <u>now</u>.'

I had no choice but to keep walking – every time I stopped Jason would thump me, words and insults continuing to spill out of his insane mouth.

'I knew from that first moment that Georgey would be SOFT. Full of wind and puff; mushy like a slug. *Glutinous* George. *Gummy* George. *Gooey* George. Pompous and proud – one hundred per cent full of himself.'

I couldn't speak from pain and fear. Eventually we reached the top of a hill – a sharp drop in front of us. I was angry and desperate, straining to think of a way to escape. Jason had obviously been looking for this sort of spot and I was terrified as to his logic. It was the first time I had a chance to understand that I was going to die aged sixteen.

He was eaten up with hatred of me. Then he openly confessed to poisoning Matt on the plane.

'I did it all to <u>perfection</u>. I went to the toilet and opened up the two packets. It was like a scientific investigation. I crushed up the peanuts very small, little more than dust. I tell you, that was the most exciting bit of all. Then I sprinkled some on to the sweets. Tasty. I'M THE MASTER. I COMMAND LIFE AND DEATH.'

Jason said a million things. Much of it didn't really make sense, not in the way that things *we* would say made sense. It was all about how he hated me and wanted to kill me. But at other times he seemed to admire me as well and want to be like me. He resented everything I had done – but I couldn't make out why. He was wild. Totally mad.

Much of what happened on that hilltop was a blur to me. I was punched and kicked repeatedly.

'I'll admit – honesty, more honesty than YOU have, *remember* – that I was a little bit jealous. And it was then that my hatred began to grow. Like a beanstalk.'

He told me about his family – and how he had

suffered. He got madder and madder. What he said became crazier and crazier. I drifted in and out of consciousness.

'Look at me now. WAKE UP. WAKE UP. IT MAKES ME SO BLOODY ANGRY WHEN YOU DON'T DO WHAT I SAY. Please. Don't. Make. Me. Do. Something. **You'll.** Regret.'

I became aware that Jason was explaining everything that had happened – even details such as the stealing of Reg's clothes. He said a lot about Zara and me and how he hated that. He was mixed up.

I stared at Jason, praying that he would show pity.

'Seeing your pathetic eyes now – such sad, stupid eyes – I think that JUSTICE has been served.'

'There are people who can help you,' I mumbled.

'WHAT WAS THAT? Did I hear you say something? GO ON – I dare you to say it again. GO ON – say that right into my ear. I'm listening. WELL?'

I was struggling to think straight. 'You can stop,' I muttered. 'You don't have to murder me as well.'

'NO. I am _not_ a murderer. I am no more a murderer than a fisherman or a farmer. I WAS FORCED TO DO THIS BY GEORGEY'S BEHAVIOUR.'

But Jason spat his words back at me. He was open about Luke, his 'puppet', and how he had controlled him, forced him to try to kill me, and then turned on him and poisoned him.

'Luke was *good*. He wasn't nearly as stupid as he seemed. But then he started to have doubts – started to feel the stupidest thing in the world: GUILT. Guilt. That pathetic hand that covers your mouth and stops you breathing. Stops you living. He had to be controlled. And <u>control</u> is my business. Isn't it? <u>You</u> can hardly disagree. Given the pathetic position you're in. Come on. Let me hear you say that you agree. Let me hear you say it, Georgey. "YOU HAVE CONTROL OVER ME AND I'M HELPLESSLY UNDER YOUR TOTAL POWER."'

There were so many words that I cannot remember them all.

'YOU SEE WHAT YOU ARE DEALING WITH.'

Then Jason started talking about his accomplice.

'It worries me that you're so THICK IN THE HEAD that you can't work out who my assistant is.'

He told me about how he had killed Toby and Reg. He openly confessed. Then he spoke to his accomplice over the walkie-talkie.

'Can you hear me? Come out, come out wherever you are. Come out, come out wherever you are . . .'

Time was a blur, but it probably didn't take that long for Peter to arrive. Yes, Peter. I was shocked too. He can't have been far behind us, maybe only an hour or so.

Then Jason told me that Peter was no longer useful to him – that he was going to become another victim.

'Greater love hath no man than he who lays down his friend for his life. So you may want to look away when he arrives. Because it'll be BYE-BYE. And then we'll be alone at last and I CAN DESTROY YOU AND BE KING.'

When Peter came towards me, he grinned, then kicked me a couple of times – but almost immediately Jason turned on him.

'Peter Pan, you've played your part and now it's time to EXIT. It's time for you to fly with the other Lost Boys. I have to be here alone with him – that's the plan. It's our destiny. Come this way and you can leave in a civilized manner. No. Don't try to struggle. DON'T YOU DARE TRY TO STRUGGLE! You've done your work and now YOU HAVE TO GO. LET'S GO TO THE EDGE TOGETHER. COME ON. I'll go over with you if you like. Really, I will. If that's what it takes.'

Peter was as tall as Jason but had nowhere near the muscle or weight, but he did fight. Peter was edged closer and closer to the drop.

'GOING, GOING, GONE!'

When this happened, I knew that I would soon follow. Jason seemed to think everything was a joke.

'How many lives have you saved? Not as many as I have finished. I win. How I hate you. BUT WANT WHAT YOU HAVE. You're just a stinking thief, people like you, stealing from people like me. Your fancy family and cosy house and girlfriend – girlfriend<u>s</u> wanting you to do things to them. WHY NOT ME? WHY NOT ME? WHY NOT ME? <u>But from now on it will be me.</u> SAY SORRY BEFORE IT IS ALL OVER. SORRY FOR THE THINGS YOU ARE GUILTY OF. Come on. STAND UP ON YOUR FEET AND SAY SORRY.'

I had been working on the rope that Jason had tied my hands with throughout the time that he had been talking to me, which was at least an hour – possibly two. It was loose to the point that I was sure I could free my hands if I pulled hard.

'Get up! It's time for us to be free of you at last. It's time for me to take over.'

'It's not too late for you to change your mind,' I mumbled through bloody and split lips. 'You can get help.'

'I DON'T NEED HELP. I AM THE NORMAL ONE. YOU ARE THE STRANGE ONE. I AM LIKE EVERYONE ELSE.'

Jason shook me violently, but then whispered in my ear.

'And I have left a note. An insurance policy. YOU will get the blame for everything.'

EVIDENCE #4
A NOTE LEFT IN THE SECOND HUT,
NEXT TO THE SINK, ABOUT EIGHT FEET
FROM THE BODY OF ALASTAIR BOYD

PLEASE HELP US. We are in great danger. Some of our group have been ~~killed~~ murdered and we are sure that a person on the trip is responsible. We suspect GEORGE FLEET, possibly with Matt Lough being forced or tricked to help him.

Please help us quickly. We don't know what to do.

We will try to reach the next hut, but PLEASE SEND HELP STRAIGHT AWAY.

Signed by

Jason Bayne (group leader after the murder of Toby Jones by George Fleet)

Nick McGregor

Peter Emsworth-Lyle

250

'Georgey, your fingerprints are LITERALLY over everything. And now it's time for BYE-BYE.'

It was at this moment my hands wriggled free from the rope. It was as much as I could do to restrain myself: the excitement of being free, of having a chance, leapt within me – but it was obvious that a straight fight would be hopeless. I kept my hands close together, the rope wrapped round them so that they appeared tied, and hoped for a chance.

Although I was dehydrated and mildly concussed, had two broken ribs and a fractured lower left arm as a consequence of the beating, my willpower was intense as Jason bundled me towards the drop.

I had advantages: one was surprise; and it's amazing what you can do when desperation roars inside you. I also had *anger* to avenge what had happened. I think I had a sense that justice wasn't mine to hand out, but I was driven by what had happened to Matt and felt that there was still, perhaps, some hope of saving him.

Jason shoved me to within about half a pace of the edge and put his mouth to my ear.

'THIS WAS ALL YOUR FAULT! YOU CAUSED THIS.'

He was standing alongside me, talking all the time. A stream of nonsense.

There was no dramatic fight at the edge of the drop. I simply, quickly, slid my right arm behind Jason's back and gave him one huge heave forward.

This move was a complete surprise to him. But – I will be honest – the strange thing is that he didn't punch me or grab me. Maybe he thought I wasn't capable of trying to kill him. Maybe he was weakened too. Maybe I was lucky. Maybe, just *maybe*, he let it happen. In any case, he resisted for a couple of seconds, half turning, his feet eventually sliding over the edge. For an instant we were staring into each other's eyes. Then he slipped over the edge.

I almost went with him, teetering there, nearly tipping over, waving my arms to regain my balance.

The initial drop wasn't quite sheer: there were still some rocks jutting out and Jason caught his right foot on one of these, and managed to grab hold of some tufts of yellowed weeds that were by my feet. Then his foot slipped and his left hand grabbed hold of loose rocks and dry dirt.

All I had to do was kick his right hand and he would fall.

'HELP ME. YOU'RE SUPPOSED TO BE THE HERO. YOU'RE SUPPOSED TO BE PERFECT. <u>Now you need to prove that you are perfect.</u>'

252

He did not say *I saved you, now you should do the same.* He said, 'Now you need to prove that you are perfect.' It was the calmest thing he had said for hours.

I wanted to do the right thing. But what was right?

And there I have to end. I have been advised by my lawyer to say nothing.

If I kicked away Jason's hand, I would be admitting manslaughter *at least* – I would have a chance of total acquittal, of course, but it would affect the court's understanding of the other deaths I may yet stand trial for.

I have been advised to say that Jason slipped straight over the edge – an accident. But that would be a lie.

Perhaps he threatened the girls' group and I let him drop from my clasp.

Perhaps I reached down and tried to pull him up. Perhaps he looked me in the eye and smiled and then pulled his hand away from mine, letting himself fall. But I have been advised that no one would believe that: it would make me a less credible witness. Therefore – and this is an important legal statement – I am not saying that happened.

Perhaps I can't remember what I did, and sometimes I wish I had done one thing, and sometimes another.

But it is true that Jason said, 'Georgey!' and then screamed, before hitting the rocks at the bottom.

I wonder what went through his mind as he fell. Perhaps he was sorry? Maybe he was so full of hate that he was evil until the very end?

I have to be honest: given what he did, I'm not sorry that Jason died.

I didn't look at the two bodies at the bottom of the cliff. I stumbled a few yards and collapsed.

And there I lay for nearly a day.

One important part of the story was happening about twenty miles up the river. Just think: the water that was gliding past the girls was the same stuff passing me. Apparently, Andrea had been trying to contact us, and Zara and Belle were pestering her like mad. Jason had checked in with Cairns, and lied about how things were going on our trip. But Andrea was used to getting daily calls from Toby, and Zara and Belle were convinced that Matt and I would have been keen to make contact. They didn't understand why their calls to us went unanswered.

The girls and Andrea wouldn't let it rest with the cops. And *that* is why the police investigated – and *that* is why I'm sitting here now instead of dead. [THANK YOU! Amazing!]

From a helicopter, the rangers had seen the missing kayaks and flown down the river until they saw them discarded and then found me on a nearby hilltop.

I hazily remember a helicopter landing nearby; I remember receiving medical help.

I was asked about the rest of the group.

Through tears, I said, 'There's no one left. I'm the only survivor.'

ABOUT THE AUTHOR

Tom Hoyle is the pseudonym of a London
head teacher.

ACKNOWLEDGEMENTS

Thank you to AW for encouragement and advice. Thanks also to CP and R(L)S for being first readers.

Thank you to Gillie Russell at Aitken Alexander. Again it is true that if it had not been for Gillie, nothing would have reached the printed page.

Macmillan is a wonderful publisher. Thank you to Venetia Gosling and Helen Bray for editorial changes, Sam Stewart for copy-editing, Nick de Somogyi for proof-reading, Fliss Stevens and Tracey Ridgewell for setting and layout, Cate Augustin for production, and Rachel Vale for another striking cover.

I am grateful to all involved in the process who have supported a book written not for them, but primarily for kids.

MORE CHILLING BOOKS
BY TOM HOYLE

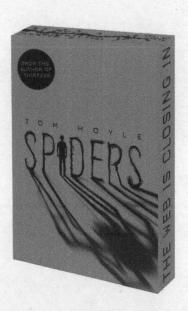

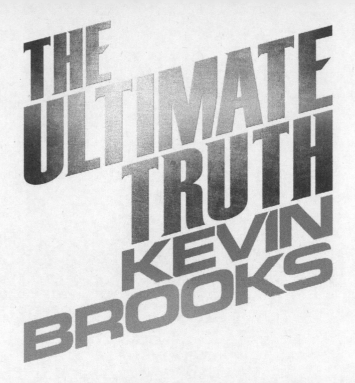

THE ULTIMATE TRUTH

KEVIN BROOKS

I HAD TO FIND OUT WHAT WAS GOING ON.
IT WAS AS SIMPLE AS THAT.
I *HAD* TO KNOW.

Travis's parents have been killed in a car crash. It looks like an accident, but Travis has his doubts. To distract himself from his grief, he goes to the private investigation agency they ran and begins asking questions about their last case. Immediately he's plunged into a mystery that seems impossible to unpick. Why were Travis's mum and dad hired to find a boy whose parents insist isn't missing? Where is the kid now? Has he run away, or is he mixed up in something sinister? And why are the CIA, MI5 and a shadowy organisation known as Omega interested in the case of a missing teenager?

TRAVIS DELANEY

THE BOX
OF
DEMONS

DANIEL WHELAN

THE APOCALYPSE BEGAN IN A SMALL SEASIDE TOWN IN WALES ...

Ben Robson can't remember a time before he had the box, with
its three mischief-making demon occupants: smelly, cantankerous
Orf, manically destructive Kartofel and fat, slobbering
greedy-guts Djinn. When Ben was a kid it was fun and he enjoyed
their company. Now he's older they're nothing but trouble.

Then one day Ben has an angelic visitor who tells him that
he can be rid of the box forever if he sends it back to hell.
There's only one catch – the box has other plans . . .